Praise for #1 *New York Times* Bestselling Author Sandra Brown

"Sandra Brown has continued to grow with every novel."
—*Dallas Morning News*

"Brown's storytelling gift is surprisingly rare, even among crowd pleasers."
—*Toronto Sun*

"A novelist who can't write them fast enough."
—*San Antonio Express-News*

"Brown's forte is devising plots spiced with sexuality that keep her readers guessing."
—*Library Journal*

"Plotting and pacing are Brown's considerable strengths."
—*San Jose Mercury News*

"A master storyteller."
—*Newport News Daily Press*

"She knows how to keep the tension high and the plot twisting and turning."
—*Fresno Bee*

"Sandra Brown is known for her memorable storytelling."
—*Tulsa World*

AND HER #1 *NEW YORK TIMES* BESTSELLER
THE ALIBI

"Murder, deceit, and passion percolate in this thriller."

—People

"*The Alibi* won't disappoint."

—Orlando Sentinel

"Probably the best work by far by this awesome author. Fast paced . . . filled with twists and turns. . . . This crisp tale proves that the best just get better."

—Harriet Klausner, *Midwest Book Review*

"A story Brown's fans will savor."

—Kirkus Reviews

"Fast paced and gripping. Chapters end with irresistible surprises, and you have to stop in the middle of one if you want to go to work or to sleep. . . . Great popular fiction . . . steamy and atmospheric . . . full of deep, dark nights and sudden silver linings . . . haunting . . . always entertaining. . . . A TRUE GREAT READ."

—Baton Rouge Magazine

"A riveting tale of conflicting loyalties."

—BookPage

TEMPTATION'S KISS

By Sandra Brown

SANDRA BROWN

TEMPTATION'S KISS

WARNER BOOKS

NEW YORK   BOSTON

Copyright © 1983 by Sandra Brown
All rights reserved. No part of this book may be reproduced in any form or by any electronic or mechanical means, including information storage and retrieval systems, without permission in writing from the publisher, except by a reviewer who may quote brief passages in a review.

This Warner Books edition is published by arrangement with the author.

Warner Books

Time Warner Book Group
1271 Avenue of the Americas, New York, NY 10020
Visit our Web site at www.twbookmark.com

Printed in the United States of America

First Warner Books Printing: January 1998
Reissued: May 2001, April 2005

10 9 8 7 6 5 4 3 2 1

Dear Reader,

For years before I began writing general fiction, I wrote genre romances. *Temptation's Kiss* was originally published more than ten years ago.

The story reflects the trends and attitudes that were popular at the time, but its themes are eternal and universal. As in all romance fiction, the plot revolves around star-crossed lovers. There are moments of passion, anguish, and tenderness—all integral facets of falling in love.

I very much enjoyed writing romances. They're optimistic in orientation and have a charm unique to any other form of fiction. If this is your first taste of it, please enjoy.

Sandra Brown

One

"*T*his is your last warning, Barnes," Megan Lambert said in a voice that made her subordinate shift uncomfortably in his chair. "To say the client was upset is putting it mildly. He said you hadn't even mentioned the country-music special to him. He would have bought as many commercial spots in that hour-and-a-half program as we would let him."

The young man squirmed uneasily and averted his eyes from her steady gaze. He cleared his throat nervously. "I just didn't think—"

Megan's palm made an unexpectedly loud crack in the still room as she slapped the top of the fruitwood desk. "That's precisely my point. You haven't been *thinking*. This is the third time I've had to reprimand you in as many weeks. Every time you pull one of these incompetent stunts, it costs this television station thousands of dollars."

She rose from her chair and went around the corner of the desk, propping her shapely hip against the corner and crossing slender ankles. "More than that, when you foul up it makes me look bad. I have to report to

1

the station manager that we aren't meeting budget and then he chews me out. Do you get my drift, Barnes?"

"Uh, yes."

"What's the problem?" she fired at him.

Her sharp tone wasn't that of a concerned parent or a sympathetic teacher, but more closely resembled that of a drill sergeant who really didn't care what the problem was, but only wanted it rectified.

Barnes looked up at her with a hopeful expression. "Well, I've been having trouble with this girl. She—"

"Spare me the details, Barnes," Megan cut in briskly. "I don't care who your current love interest is. I don't care about the status of your personal life except as it relates to your work."

She leveled her eyes on him, and he quailed under the impact. "I'll review your sales report at the end of this week. There had better be a vast improvement. And I suggest you take Mr. Thornton of Countrytime Records and Music stores to lunch and between now and then put together an advertising package that will cost us revenue but will soothe his ruffled feathers."

"Okay," he muttered.

Megan circled the corner of the desk and sat down again. Unnecessarily she thumped a stack of papers to straighten them, and said, "Now, if you'll excuse me, I have other things to do." Taking his cue, Barnes left the office, with the relief of a man being granted a stay of execution.

Rather than feeling satisfied with the scene she had

just played so well, Megan sighed wearily and slumped back in her high-backed leather chair. A well-manicured hand reached up to sweep back a wayward strand of auburn hair. She hated having to play the heavy in situations like this last one, but it was often required of her.

Standing, she walked to the wide window and opened the blinds a little wider. The skyline of Atlanta came into sharp focus, but she hardly saw it. Like all the salespeople under her supervision, she cared about Barnes, his happiness with his work, and his general well-being.

But what she had told him was true. As local sales manager for WONE TV, she had to make weekly sales reports to the station manager. If one account slipped, it cost the television station thousands of dollars in commercial time. Doug Atherton would apply the pressure expected of him. She in turn had to come down hard on her staff. It was perpetual buck-passing.

Her sympathies were with Barnes. He was heartbroken over a woman in the newsroom who had dumped him for a cameraman on the studio floor crew. Instead of complicating his life further, Megan wished she could console him, give him an opportunity to confide in her.

But she couldn't afford such a luxury, especially since she was a woman holding down a man's job and everyone more or less expected her to think with her heart instead of her head. When it came to business, she put aside her sensitive instincts and reacted to everything with pure professionalism. She didn't let personalities influence her business decisions.

Turning on the high heels of her snakeskin sandals, she studied her tastefully decorated office. She hadn't acquired it by being soft and generous. It was always difficult to let a salesperson go if he wasn't making the grade, but she had done it before and would do it again if necessary. The station management had never enjoyed sales records like the ones she'd set since becoming local sales manager, two years ago.

She hoped Barnes would come around. Not only did she want to maintain that tremendous growth in sales, but she'd always found it hard to back down once she'd taken a stand. She'd told Barnes he'd be fired unless he shaped up, and she intended to keep her promise. Many people would call her stubborn. She would have amended that definition to steadfast.

The light on her intercom panel lit up and beeped softly. She returned to her desk. "Yes, Arlene?" she said after pressing down the button that allowed her to communicate with her secretary.

"Mr. Bennett is asking to see you. Are you free?"

Instantly her body tensed into immobility. Her heart seemed to skip a beat and then pounded at double time, sending the blood roaring in her ears. For a moment she forgot to breathe, and then gasped in air until she felt dizzy. For what seemed a small eternity, she remained poised motionlessly over her desk. Then gradually she sank into her chair.

"Mr. Bennett?" The hard knot of distress that was lodged in her throat made the name sound hoarse.

"Mr. Joshua Bennett, of the Bennett Agency."

There was an undertone of puzzlement in Arlene's well-modulated voice. The Bennett Agency was responsible for a large percentage of the station's advertising clients. The largest and most prestigious in Atlanta, the agency handled clients from all over the southeastern quarter of the country. Megan knew to the cent the revenue the agency funneled into WONE's coffers, but since assuming her job, she'd never worked with Joshua Bennett directly. He knew why, and, after making a few attempts to see her, he hadn't pressed her for an interview. His agents had always worked with one of her salespeople.

Why was he asking to see her now?

Her first instinct was to make an excuse, but she squelched it. That would be cowardly, and she couldn't tolerate the thought of Joshua Bennett's considering her a coward.

"Ms. Lambert?" Arlene inquired softly.

The words should have indicated to Megan that her agitation was far too obvious. When had Arlene ever called her by anything but her first name? "Yes, all right. I can see Mr. Bennett for a few minutes."

She clicked off the intercom and tried to gather her thoughts, but they escaped from her mind like whimsical fireflies, shooting off into a million directions. She thought to stand up, then changed her mind and sat back down, her decision based largely on the seeming inability of her legs to support her. There wasn't nearly enough time to prepare herself for facing her nemesis, before he strolled through her door with all the arrogant self-assurance she remembered.

He shut the door behind him. She fell victim to eyes the color of, and as multi-faceted as, topaz. He looked at her for an interminable moment before saying softly, "Hello, Megan."

"Mr. Bennett."

Rather than seeming put down by her chilly greeting, he appeared amused. But then she remembered that everything in life seemed to amuse him. As always, his smug condescension irritated her, and the anger he'd always engendered began to simmer again. She was glad for it. At least now she was no longer held in the grip of the catatonia that had seized her the moment she'd heard his name.

She assessed him with as much objectivity as possible. Physically he hadn't changed since she'd seen him last—at her husband's funeral.

If anything, the additional silver in his dark hair made him more magnetically attractive than ever. He possessed an animal appeal that wasn't exactly sinister but certainly was dangerous. It made a woman both curious and wary, as though she would be gambling with her virtue to be left alone with him. How well

Megan knew how he used that appeal. It was all she could do to keep her lip from curling with distaste.

His tall body was still trim, hard, and powerful. Apparently he continued to work out at a gymnasium each day, while driving his employees at a pace that prevented them from taking care of themselves as well. She resented each honed muscle that curved beneath the perfectly tailored charcoal-gray suit and soft blue shirt.

He stood just inside the door with the calm self-confidence with which he handled every situation. She had no choice but to extend the common courtesy. "Won't you sit down, Mr. Bennett?"

"Thank you," he said with a scrupulous politeness that made her blood boil. Just once she wished he'd show his true colors and laugh contemptuously at the world instead of playing his cat-and-mouse game with its lowly inhabitants. She knew that was how he really felt. The universe and everyone in it were his playthings, and he toyed with them at will, like a decadent god.

His amber eyes surveyed her insolently as he sat down across from her. Slowly he analyzed the soft, cinnamon-colored hair that feathered back from her cheek and jaw. His eyes met hers for a brief moment before moving downward to her mouth and resting there for an uncomfortably long time. She was almost grateful when they continued downward, until she felt them grazing her breasts beneath the yellow voile blouse, with its dainty vertical tucks and small pearl buttons. To her horror, she felt her nipples pouting as though obeying a softy spoken command. Why hadn't she left on the jacket to her dove-gray suit?

"You're looking well, Megan."

"Thank you."

"But then, you always did," he said quickly, as if she hadn't spoken.

She made a busy project of thumbing through the folders Arlene had brought in to her earlier that morning. "I have a full schedule today, Mr. Bennett. What—"

"That's funny," he interrupted, arching an eyebrow in the manner that caused havoc in the hearts of women. A scar jagged through his eyebrow's thick curve and made it daringly masculine. "Your secretary said your calendar was open today. That's why she granted me this interview without an appointment."

Megan's jaw ached from the force with which she held it clenched. Putting down an urge to lash out at him that her calendar was none of his damn business, she asked tightly, "Is there trouble with how we're handling one of your clients' accounts?"

"No, none at all," he said easily, unbuttoning his suit coat and hoisting an ankle up to rest on the opposite knee.

His casual posture increased her vexation. If her heart was pounding and her hands were growing slippery with perspiration, the least he could do was look a little bit discomposed. Uppermost in her mind was the thought that he mustn't know how he bothered her. But he probably did know. He knew the devastating effect he had on women, and used it ruthlessly. No doubt he remembered the night when she had succumbed . . .

"Are you familiar with Seascape?" His question whipped her back into the present.

"Seascape? Yes, the new resort on Hilton Head." She wanted to compliment him on his agency's outstanding publicity for the lavish new facility on the resort island off the coast of South Carolina. Extravagant ads for the soon-to-open resort were now being seen everywhere, on billboards and in magazines. However, she refrained from expressing her appreciation. She'd never give Joshua Bennett credit for anything except destruction. "Your agency has purchased an extensive package of television-advertising time for it."

"That's what I want to talk to you about."

Her heart plummeted to the pit of her stomach. The amount of television time sold to Seascape had been astronomical. Was he going to withdraw a chunk of it? All of it? It would be just like him to do something so perverse. He had been accused of being many things, but predictable wasn't one of them.

Megan had confidence in her abilities. She'd been given the sales-manager job two years ago because of her sales record. There was untold pressure associated

with the job, both from petulant clients and impossible-
to-please management. If she met one budget, even
surpassed it, they gave her a higher one. Yet she had
handled every challenge capably.

She had control over those matters. But some
aspects of her job she couldn't control. The economy,
for instance. Or decisions made by other people. If the
NFL players went on strike and there was no football
season, she lost thousands of dollars in revenue from
clients who would have advertised on the football
games. She also had no control over the dirty politics
that were sometimes involved.

If Joshua Bennett arbitrarily pulled that plum of an
account out from under them, there would be little she
could do about it. Unless he made a demand of her.
She shuddered even to think about what that demand
might be.

With all the cool detachment she could muster, she
said, "Well?"

He grinned sardonically, that lopsided, satanic grin
that he must know would be sexually arousing to a
woman who was less discriminating than Megan. "Ms.
Hampson is handling the account for WONE."

"She's very good." Megan came immediately to the
defense of her employee.

"Yes, she is. She's a very charming young woman."

Megan reflected on Jo Hampson's lush figure and
bubbling personality and could well imagine how
"charming" Joshua Bennett must find her.

"But she's young and doesn't inspire the confidence Terry Bishop needs at this point."

"You're referring to the developer of Seascape." Megan recalled Jo Hampson's mentioning the designer and builder by name.

"Yes. He's a genius at a drafting board, with a pencil in his hand and visions in his head, but as a businessman he needs constant guidance. He's created a virtual paradise on Hilton Head and he's been granted unlimited funds to promote it. Money's no problem, but I've had to spoon-feed him every step of the way on marketing the total-resort concept."

"If you're personally in charge on his account, Mr. Bennett, I'm sure there can't be any serious problems."

Irritation thinned his lips before he forced another grin. "Thank you, but Mr. Bishop needs a second opinion. A consultation, if you will." He leaned forward in his chair, all business now. "I want you personally to handle the account for Seascape."

Their eyes locked and held over the soft patina of her desk top, and for a moment they were no longer talking about Seascape. Instead Megan was drawn back in time to the night he had pinned her against the latticed wall of a gazebo and said, "I want you to kiss me and then tell me that you love James Lambert."

"I can't," she said now with the same uncertainty with which she had answered him then. She licked her lips and tore her eyes away from the seductive power of his gaze. "I can't. This account means a big commission to Ms. Hampson. She's doing well. I can't just pull her off the account for no valid reason."

He sat back in his chair. "I'm not asking you to. I only want you to oversee it more closely. I want Jo to check every decision with you before she acts on it. I want you to meet Terry Bishop and reassure him that the commercials already produced are superb."

"If he doesn't trust your opinion, why should he trust mine?"

"Because I've told him how damn good you are," he said sharply, finally giving vent to the impatience she had known lay close to the surface.

His words took her aback, and she jumped to her feet, going to the window for the second time that morning. The sun had disappeared behind a cloud, and the city suddenly looked dreary. How apropos, she thought. The day had started badly, with her confrontation with Barnes. Now Josh Bennett had further disturbed her peace. Still, she couldn't help but bask in a small light of pride that he considered her opinion worth so much. "Why would you tell him I'm so good?" she asked.

"Because it's true. He trusts your judgment. As do I. At least in business matters." She heard him stand up, and panicked when his footsteps came close behind her. "I'm proud of what you've accomplished."

"Well, don't be," she said waspishly, whirling around. It alarmed her to find him standing so close. She had to tilt her head up to look at him. She'd forgotten just how tall he was. He always seemed to tower over her. Her husband, James, had been short, much more complementary to her petite height. If nothing else, Josh's sheer size terrified her. "I don't want to hear any patronizing praise for the poor little widow struggling in the cold cruel world," she said. "Especially not from you."

"I'm not patronizing you, damn it. My people tell me that if they always worked with a sales force as competent as yours, they'd have no problems."

"Thank you," she said stiffly, conceding to let him flatter the people working under her.

"Why wouldn't you consent to see me after the funeral?" The unexpected question struck her in the heart like a bullet, opening up a wound that had refused to heal in three years. "You wouldn't return my calls. You didn't answer my notes. Why?" he demanded.

She stepped away and glared up at him with undisguised hatred. "I didn't want to, that's why. I found your insincere bereavement at James's funeral ludicrous and wanted no part of your hypocrisy."

The muscles in his jaw flexed and hardened. The irises of his eyes glinted like amber glass. "When James collapsed in his office, I administered CPR myself. When that didn't work, I drove him to the hospital, not even waiting for an ambulance. I did everything possible to save his life. He was my good friend, my best employee. How can you reasonably say that I wasn't grieved by his death?"

"Because you did your best to kill him."

"You know better than that, Megan."

"No, I don't. The long hours you demanded, brought on his coronary. He was thirty-five years old!" she shouted. "Men that age don't drop dead of heart attacks unless they're under intense, insurmountable pressure. I would think guilt alone would have made you too ashamed to come to the funeral, much less mouth your insincere platitudes to me afterward."

"Guilt?" His irregular eyebrow cocked over his eye. "Guilt over what? What's the real issue here, Megan?" Spoken softly, the question was all the more deadly. "I didn't force James to smoke five packs of cigarettes a day. I didn't insist that he take a different client to a three-martini lunch five times a week. It wasn't my fault that he didn't exercise. What do I have to feel guilty about?"

Lord, she wished she'd never broached the subject. She couldn't—wouldn't—look at him. Did he know that her heart was thudding painfully against her ribs, that only part of her agitation was due to her anger over what they were discussing? He was standing so damn close! He smelled so healthfully masculine. Each time he spoke, she drew his breath into her body like a disciple of hedonism.

"Nothing," she said. "You don't have anything to feel guilty about. I only want you to leave me alone."

He leaned toward her like a jungle cat moving in for the kill. "What do I have to feel guilty about, Megan? We're not talking about the work James did for me, and we both know it. We're talking about the night before you married him."

"No!"

"Yes," he said, grasping her upper arm before she could turn away from him. "That's what all this animosity boils down to: those few stolen minutes in the summerhouse. After you and James were married, you avoided me like the plague. If you could help it at all, we never even saw each other. You've been angry ever since that night, Megan."

"Yes," she hissed. "Why shouldn't I avoid you after the despicable thing you did to me and to your friend, James?"

He leaned over her until his mouth was mere inches from hers. His warm breath was a fragrant, moisture-laden vapor that taunted her lips. "You're not angry with me because I kissed you. You're angry because you liked it so much."

Blinding rage stunned her into immobility. For ponderous seconds she only stared mutely up at him. Then the import of his words registered with full force, and she yanked her arm free of his strong fingers and shoved herself away.

"Get out of my office, Mr. Bennett. Get out of my life." Her chest was heaving, and, to her further outrage, he seemed fascinated by the movement of her breasts beneath the fragile cloth covering them.

When at last he dragged his eyes to her face, he said, "I'll go. For now. But be honest with yourself, Megan, and admit that I'm right. You've been nursing this insane anger for years. You'd better be careful of it. Since it's self-directed, it could also be self-destructive."

Long, unhurried strides carried him to the door. With one hand on the knob, he turned back. She stood rigid, her fists balled at her sides, her spine as stiff and straight as a crowbar. "I'll be in touch," he said, and he stepped out the door, closing it quietly behind him.

When Megan relaxed her rigidly held muscles long minutes later, she had to catch herself to keep from crumpling onto the floor. She staggered toward her desk and, propping herself over it with one arm, fumbled with the buttons on the intercom with the other trembling hand. "Arlene, please hold my calls. I . . . headache. I'm going to rest for a while."

"Are you all right?" Arlene asked with immediate concern.

"Yes, yes," Megan hurried to assure her. She didn't want anyone to know how much Josh's visit had upset her. "I'm going to take an aspirin. I'll be fine."

"That's the first time you've met Mr. Bennett, isn't it?"

"No," she said slowly, after considering telling a lie. "My husband worked for him."

"I didn't know that. He's something, isn't he?" Arlene asked breathlessly.

Megan's lips hardened bitterly. "Yes, he's something."

Her knees felt rubbery as she walked toward the long sofa that took up a portion of the wall opposite her desk. Slipping off her sandals, she lay down on the nubby, oatmeal-colored upholstery and closed her eyes, trying to block out the image of Josh's face and everything he'd said.

Her thoughts were random and nebulous, but eventually they merged and came into sharp focus around the night she wished could be erased from her life— the night before she married James Lambert.

Her mother and stepfather had rented a large room at the country club for the party in honor of their daughter's marriage to James, a young advertising agent she had met while selling commercial time for a local radio station. He worked for the Bennett Agency, and the future looked bright for the young couple, who happily greeted their guests between turns around the dance floor and trips to the champagne fountain.

Megan would always remember her dress. She'd never worn it again but had hung it in the corner of a closet in her mother's house. She'd never wanted to see it after that night, though it had been beautiful. The sea-green color reflected her green eyes. The soft fabric clung alluringly to the gentle curves of her petite figure, hanging straight from a halter neckline.

Jeweled combs had held her hair in a soft topknot, and she'd worn her diamond engagement ring on the third finger of her left hand.

"James, for heaven's sake calm down," she chided laughingly as he paced the room before the party began, checking this and that, pestering the hired help by constantly getting in their way.

He hugged her enthusiastically. "How can I calm down? Tomorrow I'm going to marry the most beautiful girl in the world." She smiled, pleased, but her grin collapsed when he added, "Besides, I haven't had a cigarette in three days."

"Oh, James, you're doing so well," she said encouragingly. "And you promised to quit."

"I know, I know," he said, kissing her quickly. "I will. But if I find a smoker here tonight, I may stand beside him and breathe in real deep."

She had tolerated his hyperactivity that night. He drank too many glasses of champagne, but she didn't scold him, knowing he was drinking to compensate for not smoking. She loved his smiling face, his exuberance, his unflagging enthusiasm for life, his boundless energy, his ambition.

She had thought the tributes he paid to the owner of the Bennett Agency a trifle overblown, but when Joshua Bennett walked into the flower-bedecked room, Megan had to admit that James's acclaim wasn't unwarranted. The man certainly made a startling first impression. Tall, slender, and distinguished in his tuxedo, he exuded confidence and charm.

She felt the first tinglings of sensation when, at James's introduction, Josh Bennett's amber eyes subjected her to a thorough appraisal. But those tinglings were only harbingers of the currents that sizzled along her nerves when he took her hand and pressed her fingers lightly. She all but jerked her hand out of his electrifying clasp.

"I'm pleased to meet you, Mr. Bennett. James has told me so much about you." Somehow she had squeezed the words past her constricting throat.

"Not nearly as much as he's told me about you," he said in a confidential whisper. "And my name's Josh."

If voices could have color, his would be whiskey-colored, like his eyes. His voice was husky, mellow, and rich, like the finest bourbon.

Lulled by the sound and drawn into the maelstrom of his eyes, she all but forgot James, who was boisterously greeting a group of his former fraternity brothers.

"Say, Josh, will you dance with my girl while I show these degenerates where the real booze is kept?" James asked his employer.

Panicked, Megan watched James's neglectful retreat, knowing even then that she shouldn't be alone with Josh Bennett. Strong intuition telegraphed disaster. She didn't heed it. Had she minded her instincts then, she might not have had to pay so dearly later.

"Shall we?" he asked. His brow lifted in query, and she noticed the scar for the first time.

Before she verbalized a reply, she was pulled into the circle of his arms, and speech became impossible. He maneuvered them around the dance floor with animal grace, never faltering in matching his steps to the beat of the music.

Megan could never recall afterward what tune they had danced to. Her thoughts were centered on the hand pressing, not against her lower back, where the fabric of her dress would have provided some protection, but higher, where her skin was naked and vulnerable beneath the gentle pressure of his hand. Instead of holding her hand indifferently, he had laced their fingers loosely together. His thumb lazily stroked the side of her index finger.

He didn't hold her inappropriately close, but each time she brushed against him, her body reacted shamelessly. She hoped fervently that he didn't notice the tightening of her nipples beneath the clinging gown, or the way her thigh had found it so amenable to nest between his, or the sudden rushing of her breath in and out of her body. Not daring to meet his eyes, she stared at the onyx studs between the starched pleats of his white shirtfront.

When the song was over and Josh returned her to her fiancé, she all but fell into James's arms. Had he been rescuing her from cruel, violent ravishment, she couldn't have been more relieved to see him.

But she had been violated in a far different and much more subtle way than rape. Her heart had been debauched.

She'd wanted so badly to enjoy the evening of celebration, but Joshua Bennett's presence had ruined it for her. She was tense and nervous. Every time she ventured to glance around the room, she found his eyes drilling into her. Never able to disregard their hypnotism, she stared back at him while unthinkably erotic pictures were being painted on her mind.

The next time he asked her to dance, she accepted under the duress of James's coaxing. Her fiancé's eyes were unusually bright, and Megan knew he'd made several trips to the bar with his fraternity brothers. She gave him a disappointed look when she saw the cigarette dangling from his lips.

He shrugged engagingly. "After the wedding, I promise. Now go dance with my boss. He might give me a raise."

The band played a vigorous number that didn't require her and her partner to touch. Caught up in the drumming rhythm of the music, she smiled easily at Josh, who took to this kind of dancing with the same agility as he had the slower rhythm. Only when their hips bumped together accidentally did Megan's feet miss a beat—at the same time that her heart did. For a split second she stood stock still.

"Are you all right?" Josh asked, placing a concerned hand on her bare shoulder.

She nodded dumbly just as the band went into a slow ballad. Without asking her permission, he drew her into a warm embrace. "This is more to my liking," he murmured. His lips moved against her hair. "I like to feel a woman's body against mine . . . when I'm dancing."

Right then, then, with that first innuendo, she should have pulled away from him, politely excused herself, and not had anything more to do with him for the rest of the evening.

But she hadn't. Instead she had obeyed the imperceptible encouragement of his hand on her back and moved closer. It *did* feel good dancing body to body, especially if the other body was like this one, hard and taut, virile and warm. They swayed to the music. Megan's eyes closed languidly. Their hearts beat together. His powerful thighs moved against hers. His hips . . . Oh, God!

"I . . . excuse me," she said hoarsely. His startled arms fell away as she slipped out of them.

With what she knew was a grotesque parody of a smile plastered on her face, she wended her way through the dim room, dodging her mother, her fiancé, and anyone else who might read her guilty expression.

She needed air. She rarely drank, and she'd had too many glasses of champagne. They had gone straight to her head and made her a little crazy. Night air would clear up her head and she'd stop having these ridiculous fantasies about the man with the dark hair, golden eyes, and magnificent body, who stirred her like no man ever had.

She reveled in the cool night breeze as she circumnavigated the subtly lit swimming pool and sought privacy in the white lattice gazebo. She sank onto the bench inside the octagonally shaped structure.

Covering her face with shaking hands, she tried vainly to get a grip on herself. If only her heart would stop racing. She felt each pounding pulse at her temples, in her earlobes, in the tips of her breasts, and in the region that felt heavy and swollen and hot between her thighs.

But her heart didn't slow. Rather, it lurched and came to a dead standstill when she heard the crunch of footsteps on the gravel walkway outside. There was no doubt in her mind who the looming silhouette in the moonlit opening of the gazebo belonged to. He passed under the arch and came to her slowly through the shadows.

Galvanized by her fear of the man and her reactions to him, she bolted off the bench and tried to slip past him, but he caught her against his solid length. "Why are you marrying James Lambert?"

"I love him," she cried desperately.

"Do you?"

"Yes, of course. Yes."

"You don't sound sure."

I was. I was sure until an hour ago. "I love him. I'm marrying him tomorrow. Now, please let me go."

He did just the opposite. He held her tighter to him and walked her backward, until she was against the filagreed wall of the summerhouse. Moonlight seeping through the narrow slats cast waffle patterns on his features. "I want you to kiss me and then tell me that you love James Lambert."

"I can't," she said hoarsely. Even then she didn't know if she was saying she couldn't kiss him, or if, once she did, she wouldn't be able to tell him she loved James. She had no time to reason it through before his mouth claimed hers with heart-stopping precision.

Now, more than four years later, lying on the couch of her executive office and recalling that night, she could still vividly remember how effortlessly he'd taken possession of her mouth. His lips had been ardent but tender as they moved over her less-skilled ones. How sweetly his tongue had broken the barrier of her lips and teeth. How wonderfully thorough it had been as it explored her mouth, performing a mating dance with her own tongue.

His hands had cupped her jaw, tilting her head back for a deeper kiss, which had robbed her of conscience and scruples. His tongue left no part of her mouth intact but touched all of it, penetrating even what had until then been virgin territory.

One hand caressed her. With his thumb on one side, and his fingers on the other, he defined the underside of her breast. Lifting it slightly, he found the full nipple worthy of his attention. When his thumb began to slide along it, Megan's head fell back, and a sigh of ecstasy echoed in the night.

As his lips greedily partook of her throat, that talented thumb found the peaking desire of her breast and circled it mesmerizingly.

"Lord, you're sweet. So sweet. I knew you would be. Give me your mouth again."

Thinking about it now, Megan's fingers clenched in self-loathing as she remembered how docilely she'd offered her mouth for his carnal pleasure. And it hadn't been only his mouth that had kissed her. His body had moved along hers in one tantalizing kiss. His hard chest had pressed against her breasts. His thighs had brushed, lingered, separated, brushed again, stayed. His hand had opened wide on the small of her back and smoothed downward to cradle her hips. Holding her that way, he'd rubbed the rigid flesh in the front of his trousers against her with the same provocative motion of his tongue inside her mouth. Some demonic element in her soul had enticed her to answer with a lifting motion of her own.

"Megan, Megan," he had whispered. "You don't love James, when you can kiss me like this."

His words were like an icy deluge on her fired spirit. She swatted at the hand caressing her breast and was ashamed at feeling bereft at its loss. At the same time the heel of her other hand pushed against his chest until he stumbled backward.

"You slimy . . . Oh, to think I . . . How could you do

this to your *friend*? How could I . . . You're disgusting."

Whirling away in a cloud of sea-green chiffon, she had wiped his kisses off her mouth with the back of her hand and run out into the darkness.

Megan sat up now, feeling all the hatred for the man she had felt that night. He had no sense of propriety, shame, or moral conscience. Selfishly he went after whatever he wanted. Not that he'd wanted her, except maybe for a weekend fling. But he'd proved what he'd set out to, that he could make James Lambert's fiancée melt beneath his practiced kisses and caresses.

"What did it avail you, Mr. Bennett?" she asked now into the empty office. "I despised you then. I despise you now, and with more cause."

The buzzer on her intercom sounded again. Hauling herself up, suddenly exhausted and lethargic beyond comprehension, she crossed the room to answer it.

"Sorry to bother you, but Mr. Atherton called," Arlene informed her. "As soon as you return from lunch, he wants to see you. He said it was important."

"I'll be there," Megan replied listlessly.

Checking her watch, she saw that she had over an hour to prepare herself for the meeting with the station's general manager. She had a fairly good idea that the important matter he needed to see her about was Joshua Bennett.

Two

Megan's footsteps were silent on the lush hallway carpet. Here there were no constantly ringing telephones, scurrying reporters, clacking typewriters, and squawking police radios, as in the newsroom. Downstairs, engineers, who kept the television station on the air, worked in dim rooms full of whirring computers and lighted dials. Directors and producers used cubicles near the cavernous studios that were cluttered with scripts, storyboards, and timetables.

But this floor, which housed the executive offices of WONE, could have been found in any major corporation building in the country. This quiet hallway didn't even bear resemblance to the one in which Megan and her salespeople were pigeonholed. Her office was nicer than most of the others, because she had decorated it herself, at her own expense, but it wasn't luxurious like the one she now entered through double oak doors.

"Hi," she greeted Mr. Atherton's secretary. "Is he back from lunch?"

"Back and waiting for you." The woman smiled. "Go on in."

Pretending a confidence she didn't feel, Megan crossed the outer office and entered the sanctum where the station manager made all the major decisions regarding the television station.

"Come in, Megan," he said, making half an effort to stand as she took the deep, plush chair on the other side of his enormous desk. "Coffee?"

"No, thank you, Doug. I just had my daily carton of yogurt for lunch. I'd better let it settle."

Doug Atherton, balding and paunchy, shuddered. "God, if I ate that stuff, it would never settle." The most attractive thing about the middle-aged man was his melodious Southern drawl. Even when he was reading the riot act to an unfortunate employee, Doug's voice sounded soothing. He studied his thumbnail as he asked, "How are things in local sales this week?"

"We're above budget, I'm glad to report. I had to call Barnes in on the carpet this morning and give him a pep talk. I think—hope—he'll shape up."

"You'd better have everyone fired up. I got word that a group of bigwigs from the parent company is coming down in a few weeks. I'm sure they'll want to increase your budget."

"What else is new?" she asked dryly.

Doug nodded absently. "I'm sure you won't disappoint us. And you certainly won't want to do anything between now and their visit that could cost us an account." He cleared his throat. "Megan, Josh Bennett came to see me this morning."

The muscles of her stomach tightened, but she kept her expression impassive. "And?"

"And," he said, drawing out the word, "he wants you personally to handle this Seascape account."

"So he told me." She shifted in her seat and rested her arms on the chair in a vain attempt to appear calm. "I don't see the need of that. I have every confidence in Jo Hampson."

"Yes, but the client doesn't," Doug replied. His muddy eyes stabbed into her for a moment before his expression relaxed into one of tolerance. "I know why you have an aversion to him, Megan."

She laughed shortly. "Aversion is too soft a word, Doug. I hate him. He worked my husband to death. How else should I feel about him?"

"I knew James, and I don't think he needed a slave driver. That young man had more energy than anyone I've ever met. An excessive amount. As a matter of fact, he did everything in excess." He held both palms out when she began to object. "Wait. I'm not here to speak disrespectfully of him. It's just that I think you've blinded yourself to the facts, or at least colored them in your mind."

"Are you saying that I imagined all the late hours James worked, the endless cocktail parties, deadlines, querulous clients?" Suddenly the air in the room was stifling, the chair confining, and she pushed out of it. Circling it, she braced her hands on its padded back as she said, "I watched my husband digging his own grave because that man wouldn't let up on him. Don't ask me to feel benevolent toward Josh Bennett."

"Would it be impossible for you to work with him on this account?"

"Absolutely. In my opinion he's never done anything meritorious. He's an opportunist, a manipulator, a taker."

Doug sighed and ran a weary hand over his fleshy features. "Sit down, Megan." When she hesitated, he raised imperious eyes to her. "Sit down."

Realizing that his words were more than a request, she resumed her previous seat. Instinctively, and for a reason she couldn't name, her heart began to pound with misgiving. She had a strong premonition that she didn't want to hear what Doug was about to say.

"Megan, there's something you should know, something I probably should have told you a long time ago. Josh Bennett was responsible for your being hired at WONE."

Her instinct to be afraid had been well founded, but she couldn't have anticipated the devastating impact of Doug's words. She stared at him in stunned dismay, hoping desperately that she hadn't heard him right. His eyes looked almost pained. His expression was almost compassionate. He wasn't lying.

She tried to record and digest what he'd just told

her, but she couldn't. It was unthinkable. That she owed the man she hated most in the world her *job,* her entire life as it was today, was beyond belief.

"That's impossible," she said. "I applied for a job here on a whim."

"Even so."

Gaining strength, her reason gradually returning, she thought back to the days following James's death, three years ago. "I went back to the radio station, but they didn't need anyone. Then I applied here. How could Bennett have known?"

Atherton's shoulders lifted and fell in an eloquent shrug. "Grapevine. You know what it's like around here. Someone blows his nose and everyone knows about it. If you'll recall, when you applied we told you there was nothing available. There wasn't."

"You called me back a week later and told me you'd reconsidered my application."

"Yes, after having been paid a visit by Bennett. He was adamant, Megan. He threatened to advise all of his clients already advertising on this station to spend their money elsewhere if we didn't hire you for our sales force. He personally reviewed the account list we gave you to make sure you were being assigned a fair share of the better ones."

"My God," she whispered, covering her face with her hands.

Atherton barked a short laugh. "Bennett wields just about that much power. I wanted to tell him to go to hell, but he could make good his threats and cost us a fortune in lost advertising. Oh, yes, once I had my little chat with Bennett, I agreed to hire you in a minute."

He leaned forward and placed his folded hands on the desk. "But, Megan, I wasn't disappointed. I told Mr. Bennett that if you couldn't cut it, you'd be out in six months. He agreed to those terms. You've proven yourself, just as he assured me you would."

Megan disregarded the compliment. "He didn't even know anything about me!" she almost screamed. "He still doesn't. When James was in his employ, I had as little to do with him as possible."

Atherton shrugged again. "He made it his business to know as much as he could about you. And everything he claimed to know was accurate."

Springing to her feet again, she paced the room restlessly. She felt like a caged beast with the walls closing in. Another thought struck her, and she turned toward her supervisor. "When the job for local sales manager became available, did he have anything to do with my getting the promotion!" Her threatening gaze forbade him to lie to her.

He shook his head. "No. Management had already decided you were the one to take over. Your sales record was outstanding, and you had the necessary leadership qualities. You'd always been able to handle even the most difficult clients."

"Thank—"

"But," he cut in, "Bennett called me to suggest

strongly that you be appointed to the vacated position. I was glad I could tell him we had already reached that decision."

"He knew even before I did," she said in a voice that was deadly quiet.

Atherton paused before cautiously concurring. "Yes."

"Damn!" She pounded the arms of the chair and slumped back into the deep cushions, overcome by dejection. Atherton allowed her a few moments of introspection. Her thoughts were so tumultuous that she wasn't even aware of him until he cleared his throat softly.

"In light of what I've told you, do you think you'd reconsider Mr. Bennett's request that you handle the Seascape account?"

Her chin rose defiantly. "What is so all-fired important about that account? He doesn't need it. He's mentioned in the newspaper every day for having given money to this charity or another, attending this benefit or another. Why should he care so much about this one account?"

"Because he's a professional," Atherton shot back. "He doesn't let personal feelings stand in the way of sound business conduct."

"And I suppose you think I do," she said heatedly.

"Yes, I do!" he shouted. "Where he's concerned, yes. For the first time I'm disappointed in you. You're not approaching this in a professional manner."

That hurt. Because it was the truth, it hurt all the more. She tried to stare down Atherton and couldn't. When she lowered her eyes, he said briskly, "Can I tell him that you've consented to having dinner with him and Bishop tonight? Ms. Hampson has been asked to go too."

Dinner. With him. With Josh Bennett. She had no choice, and she knew it. Without laying it on the line, Atherton, as her superior, was telling her she must put her personal feelings aside for the sake of her career.

She stood up with straight shoulders and a tense rigidity to her mouth. "Very well."

"Good," Atherton said curtly, rummaging for something on his desk. "Here, he left this for you." He extended to her a cream-colored business card with the hateful name embossed on it. "I'll expect a report tomorrow morning."

"You'll have it."

When she reached the door, he stopped her. "Megan, this account wouldn't make or break Bennett. He's already proven himself. Maintaining the reputation of his company as the best is what motivates him. To him it's all a game, and money is only the means with which to keep score. But the Seascape commercials will mean a tremendous amount of money to us. I know you'll do a good job of keeping everyone happy."

"That's right. I will," she said archly, and proudly exited the office.

*   *   *

The personal, singular J at the end of the terse message galled her the most. Lying in bed, trying to relax after battling Atlanta's afternoon rush-hour traffic, she read the writing on the back of the business card for the hundredth time. "A car will pick you up at seven-thirty. J."

"Well, I might not want one of your damn cars to pick me up at seven-thirty, Mr. Bennett," she said aloud. But the car would arrive on time, and she knew she'd be ready. Like it or not, she had been coerced into cooperating with Josh.

After her meeting with Doug Atherton, she had spent the rest of the afternoon trying to sort out what he had divulged. She had never entertained a thought that Josh could have manipulated her life. Why had he gone to all that trouble on her behalf? Was he only trying to relieve his conscience over James's untimely death, to absolve himself of blame? That must be it. But to think she owed her success to him . . .

No! she decided, jumping from the bed and entering the bathroom for a quick shower. He might have been responsible for getting her the job in the first place, but she'd made a success of it on her own. He'd had nothing to do with that. He hadn't been there to advise her on business decisions.

Still, how was she going to face him, knowing that she owed him so much? Were it not for him and the clout he wielded, she could be struggling to live on

James's inadequate insurance and the meager salary she would have earned at a small, insignificant radio station. Instead she was sales manager of a reputable television station in one of the country's major television markets. Few women could boast that. Few *men* could.

She would face him with pride and cool disdain, she decided as she stepped into the dress she'd selected for the evening. She was going first class, just as she knew Josh would. The dress was starkly simple. Her petite figure would have been smothered by ruffles, big sleeves, or full skirts. She'd chosen all of her clothes with those limitations in mind.

Now, eyeing herself in the mirror, she knew that this dress was one of her best. The silk was a shade too soft to be pure white. The collar dipped down to a deep V that was connected to the wide self-belt at her waist by a trail of tiny rhinestone buttons. The hem of the trim skirt brushed her legs just below the knee. Her shapely calves were shown off by high-heeled, strappy sandals.

A curling iron had restored the waves falling freely on either side of her face. She placed small diamond studs in her ears and was ready. Since the dress was sleeveless, she selected a lacy shawl, and a satin evening bag. No sooner had she misted herself with a flowery perfume than her doorbell rang.

A uniformed chauffeur was standing on the threshold. "Mrs. Lambert?"

"Yes."

She stepped out, closed and locked the door behind her, and let the stately man escort her to the sleek black limousine. As soon as he'd been assured of her comfort in the posh backseat, he concentrated on his driving, leaving Megan to her own thoughts. Her dread of the coming hours so consumed her thoughts that she was surprised when the limousine cruised to a stop under the awning of one of Atlanta's finest restaurants.

When the chauffeur opened her door, the first person she saw was Jo Hampson, who waved gaily and rushed over to her. "Hi. I was glad to hear you were coming tonight. I was afraid either Mr. Bishop or Mr. Bennett would ask me something I couldn't answer."

"You could have handled it," Megan assured her.

"Thanks for the compliment, but just the same, I'm glad to have you here, boss."

They laughed easily together as the doorman ushered them inside. Dressed in pink taffeta, her blond hair a tumble of curls and her face wreathed in a guileless smile, Jo Hampson looked like a frothy strawberry confection. Next to her, Megan felt elegant and sophisticated.

Josh Bennett had a penchant for elegance, as was obvious when he came forward to greet them. He spoke a friendly greeting to Jo, but his eyes burned into Megan's as he curled his fingers around her elbow.

"I'm glad you could join us on such short notice, Megan."

She ground her teeth in an effort not to remind him she'd had no choice in the matter. Instead she replied with cool politeness, "Thank you for the invitation."

He seemed amused by her slightly sarcastic words. His finely molded lips tilted at one corner. "Mr. Bishop is already here. This way." He led them to a circular, tufted vinyl booth in a corner of the dimly lit bar.

A slender, middle-aged man with mussed gray hair and thick eyeglasses stood up. "Hello, Mr. Bishop," Jo said.

"Miss Hampson, I've asked you to call me Terry," he said, taking her hand and shaking it.

"When you drop the Miss Hampson," she retorted.

He turned toward Megan expectantly. Josh took his cue. "Terry Bishop, Megan Lambert, local sales manager of WONE."

"Mr. Bishop," she said, smiling graciously and extending her hand. She liked the man immediately. She had expected a wheeler-dealer in the same league as Josh Bennett. Instead this man looked ill at ease in these extravagant surroundings. He'd probably feel more comfortable bent over his drafting board than at a business dinner.

"Call me Terry, please," he said. "I've been anxious to meet you. Josh has told me so much about you. I understand you've been friends for a long time."

Megan ignored Jo's bemused look as she slid into the booth beside Terry Bishop. "Yes, we met through my husband several years ago." Josh's looming presence behind her forced her to scoot around the booth and allow him to move in beside her. Had the steel jaws of a trap closed around her, she couldn't have felt more confined.

Terry Bishop was saying, "Yes, Josh mentioned that. Your husband's early death was tragic."

"Yes, it was," she mumbled, covering her agitation by adjusting her skirt over her knees and placing her purse and shawl between her and Josh's hard thigh. Immediately he picked them up and laid them on the far side of him. Megan shot him a warning look, but he didn't catch it. He was asking Jo what she wanted to drink.

"And you, Megan? What do you want?"

I want you to stop pressing your thigh against mine, she wanted to shout. Instead she answered with cold civility, "White wine on the rocks, please." He kept the hovering cocktail waitress waiting while he momentarily studied her mouth.

She released her pent-up breath when he turned his head and gave the waitress their order. If only he weren't so close. If only she couldn't smell his tantalizingly spicy cologne. If only he weren't so damned good-looking. If only she couldn't remember how her name had sounded on lips that had kissed her with more passion than she'd ever known. If only she couldn't remember the way his mouth had tasted as it devoured hers.

Jo launched into an animated tale about a man who

had come to her wanting to advertise his recipe for homemade bubble gum on television. His advertising budget was limited to fifty dollars. Terry was still listening avidly when the waitress returned with their drinks. "Will there be anything else, Mr. Bennett?" she crooned as she leaned down, threatening to spill an impressive bosom out of her tight black velvet weskit.

"I'll let you know," Josh responded, smiling a slanted grin that Megan knew could melt even the coldest of feminine hearts.

"Please do." She turned away with a deliberately seductive motion of her hips beneath the short red plaid skirt.

Josh chuckled as he took a sip of his scotch and water. "Whatever happened to the hard-to-get approach?"

"I would think you'd be charmed," Megan said in a vindictive whisper for his ears alone. Jo and Terry were engrossed in their own conversation.

Josh set down his glass with a decided thump. For an endless moment, impaling topaz eyes held hers, before sliding down her throat to the deep cleft under the tapering collar of her dress. "That waitress has too much of a good thing. I've always held to the idea that it's quality, not quantity, that counts."

Megan's throat constricted painfully. His eyes seemed to penetrate her clothing, stroke the most secret, sensitive places of her body, and reacquaint them with sensations she had long put to rest. Lot's wife had superb strength of character compared to Megan when he raised his eyes to hers once again. She was powerless to look away, even though Jo had launched into another story.

Josh lay a single finger on her arm as he asked softly, "Did you talk to Atherton today?" But he didn't appear to be as interested in her meeting with her boss as he was in the diamond-studded earlobe he was studying intently. He moved his finger along her arm only enough to stir the fine hairs.

"Yes," she said tightly, jerking her arm from beneath his hand.

"And?"

"I'm here, aren't I?"

"I wasn't sure you'd come. You didn't have to."

"Oh, I had to or, believe me, I wouldn't be here," she scoffed. "You knew damn well I'd come, Mr. Bennett. Don't you always get what you want? Don't you do exactly as you please?"

"No," he growled under his breath, leaning dangerously close to her. "If I'd done as I pleased four years ago, I'd have carried you off that night, made love to you until we were both senseless, and used force, if necessary, to keep you from marrying James Lambert."

Megan's pulse thundered in her ears as she stared wide-eyed into the fierce face only a breath away from hers. The resolution that carved it into a virile mask left no doubt in her mind that he meant every word.

"Furthermore, if I was doing what I wanted to at this moment, it wouldn't be engaging in this seemingly polite conversation, but thoroughly kissing that succulent mouth of yours."

"Mr. Bennett."

"What?" he virtually barked to the interrupting maître d' as he whipped his head around.

The man took a startled step backward. "Ex— excuse me, Mr. Bennett. Your table is ready," he said deferentially.

To Megan's relief, she realized that Jo and Terry had been laughing together and hadn't noticed their host's flare of temper or the residual tension that crackled between him and Megan as they proceeded to their table.

During the two-hour meal, Megan was oblivious to the sumptuous food and impeccable service. She was captivated by Josh's forceful personality. He discussed very little business and kept up a lively conversation that covered myriad topics. He was delightful to her and Jo and companionable to Terry. She saw how everyone, her late husband included, could have been blindly attracted to this man, who exuded charm and defined charisma.

At the end of one exceptionally entertaining anecdote, she found herself laughing with the others. Truly enjoying herself, she was caught completely off guard when Josh turned to face her. In a moment of rare intimacy, a powerful look passed between them. Megan felt just as she had when James first introduced them. All her senses seemed heightened now, as then. Josh ruled them all; he was their captor. It troubled her not a little that she was almost his willing prisoner.

Then, like a locomotive coming out of a dark tunnel, all the reasons she should hate him came barreling toward her and slammed into her with enormous force. She schooled her features into a stoic mask and took a sip of her cold coffee. Out of the corner of her eye she noted the irritation that fleetingly crossed his face.

"I'm so glad you'll be consulting with us on this advertising campaign," Terry Bishop said later, shaking her hand respectfully at the door of the restaurant.

"I'll be pleased to lend any expertise I can, though I think Jo and Mr. Bennett have handled your account flawlessly."

"Oh, so do I," he hurried to assure her, "but another opinion never hurts."

He said good night when the valet brought his car under the awning. Jo's bright yellow compact arrived next. She thanked Josh and waved a gay farewell to Megan. When the limousine hummed to a stop. Josh took Megan's elbow and propelled her toward it.

"I can get home on my own," she said, resisting him.

"Yes, you could, but there's no reason why you should."

He practically pushed her into the backseat. When

she turned to issue him a polite good night, she was startled to find him entering the car behind her.

"I . . . I thought you had another car here."

"No. I took a cab from the office."

"Oh."

He settled himself against the velour cushions, stretched his long legs out in front of him, loosened his tie, and unbuttoned the top button of his shirt. It was almost as if they were familiar, a couple, as if they rode together in the backseat of the limousine every day. She sat stiffly beside him, staring straight ahead.

"Are you cold?" he asked when she wrapped her shawl closer around her. Little did he know that it was a defensive gesture. She was far too aware of the length and hardness of his male frame, the width of his chest and shoulders, the tapering slimness of his hips.

"No."

"Sure?"

"Yes."

He slid his arm around her shoulders and drew her closer. His thigh pressed against hers. "Sure?" he repeated, murmuring the word in her ear. His hot breath tickled it.

"Don't," she said, trying to move away.

"Why?" His nose brushed across her cheek in a nuzzling gesture.

"Don't," she said more strenuously, casting a worried glance at the back of the driver's head. A sheet of soundproof glass separated them. She'd find no rescue there, not that he'd thwart his employer anyway. She wrested an exploring hand from her shoulder. "Stop it, Josh. You've been touching me all night. I don't like it."

He laughed deep in his throat. "Yes, you do. That's been your problem all along. You like my touch far too well."

"I did . . . do . . . not!" she cried. "The reason I'm here now is purely professional. If you're looking for a woman to manhandle, find another one. I'm sure there are many who would enjoy it."

"Not nearly as many as there are purported to be."

"I couldn't care less. And stop doing that to my neck." Idle fingers were sliding along its satiny base under her hair. Her efforts to shrug him off were to no avail.

"What about you, Megan? How's your love life?"

"I—" She was about to say she didn't have one, but seeing the foolhardiness in that, she amended, "It's satisfactory—not that it's any of your business."

"You're lying again, Megan," he said tauntingly. "I've made it my business to know all about your love life. You've been out with exactly five men in the last three years. Three of them you only went out with once. You didn't spend the night with any of them."

A flush of heat swept up from the bodice of her dress to stain her neck and face. A rage so encompassing that it frightened her filled every pore. "You—"

He silenced her by laying his index finger against

her lips. "That kissable mouth shouldn't utter the obscenities you're thinking right now. Besides that, you're home."

Before she could gather her wits, he was drawing her out of the backseat. The night air was redolent with the perfume of early summer flowers. A breeze cooled her fevered skin but not the anger boiling inside her. She was so upset that the intricacies of fitting her key in the lock defeated her.

He reached around her, plucked the key theatrically from her shaking fingers, and unlocked the door easily. In an instant they were inside the dark house and she was being pressed against the wall of the foyer.

"No!" she gasped before his mouth swooped down on hers. She fought him, pushing against the rock-hard wall of his chest, whipping her head from side to side, eluding the audacious demands of his mouth.

Manacling both her wrists in one iron fist, he raised her arms over her head and held them there. With the other hand he trapped her jaw to hold her head immobile while his lips moved over hers.

As much as she wanted to indict him for this insult, she couldn't fault him with brutality. His lips weren't hard and bruising, but soft and persuasive, as he kissed her once, twice, a third time, lingering longer with each touch of his mouth on hers.

A knot of tension deep inside her began to uncoil and spread to touch the erogenous areas of her body. Unwanted desire that had been hiding in the darkest recesses of her being ventured out, testing its freedom, wandering at will.

When Josh's tongue probed at her lips and then pushed between them to stroke along her teeth, she heard her own soft whimper of hopeless, helpless despair. Fighting it, denying it, was an exercise in futility. She wanted this man. She had always wanted him. And he knew it.

But even that untenable fact didn't prevent her from indulging in this one forbidden kiss. She'd rebuke herself later. Remorse was always reserved for later. For right now she convinced herself that it was useless to struggle against his superior strength.

He possessed her mouth jealously. His tongue plundered it until his monarchy was established unquestionably, then he kissed her with leisure. He savored the honeyed crevice of her mouth, dipping his limber tongue deeper each time to catch every sweet taste.

She stood perfectly still, not daring to participate, yet holding a tight rein on every nerve in her body that cried out for her to join this orgy of sensations. It wasn't until his hand sinuously glided down her neck and throat to begin unhooking the buttons of her bodice that she realized she was precariously close to surrender.

She dragged her mouth from under his. "No, Josh," she said, trying to twist away from him, but only succeeding in educating herself to the strength of his arousal. The hard proof of it against her soft middle alarmed her. Or was it her thrilling reaction to it that panicked her? "No!"

"Megan," he uttered in a harsh whisper as he finally released the buttons and placed his palm on the lush curve of her breast, "there's a commandment against coveting your friend's wife, and I was guilty as sin of it while you were married. I've wanted you from the first night I saw you, held you, kissed you."

His lips found the soft indentation at the base of her throat and planted ardent kisses there. His hand grew bolder, caressing her in ways that stole her breath away and elicited ripples of sensation throughout her body, sensations she hadn't felt since the last time he had touched her this way.

"I've given you time—time to heal, time to earn your own wings, time to prove yourself. But by God, my generosity just ran out."

His declaration, not to mention the fingertips slipping past the lacy border of her bra to test the degree of her own desire, both frightened and aroused her. Acting out of sheer animal instinct for self-preservation, she resisted him. Knowing that if she surrendered, she'd be irrevocably, eternally lost, she closed her heart to its own pleadings. Knowing she could never overcome him physically, she used her only weapon.

"Am I to add rape to all the other indignities you've heaped on me?"

His head snapped up as though someone had grabbed a handful of his hair and yanked it hard. His raspy breathing echoed loudly off the walls of the still house as he met her accusing gaze.

If she had expected contrition, she couldn't have been more wrong. Angrily he brought her arms down and hauled her against him.

"I want you, and I'll have you. There's no doubt in my mind, or in yours, of the final outcome. The sooner you come around, the better for both of us."

His scorching kiss was as much an assault on her senses as on her pride. Then, releasing her abruptly, he said a curt "Good night" and slammed the door behind him, leaving her alone in the entryway feeling utterly bereft.

Three

Only a moment after Megan entered her office the next morning, she was storming back through the door, confronting her secretary. "Where did those come from?" she demanded. Her pointing finger could leave no doubt what she was referring to. Arranged in a tall lead-crystal vase on her desk were two dozen roses interspersed with fern and baby's breath. That the roses were her favorite shade, a peachy pink color, made her unaccountably incensed.

"The roses?" Arlene queried, obviously perplexed by Megan's vexation.

"Yes, the roses."

"They were delivered."

"When?"

"About ten minutes ago. There's a . . . uh . . . card."

Without another word, Megan closed her office door stridently behind her and marched toward her desk. The vase hadn't come from a florist. It had been bought elsewhere and taken to the florist to arrange the roses in. Crystal of that quality didn't come out of a flower shop.

She jerked the card from the holder and ripped it open. The singular initial leaped off the card to mock her. It was in his own handwriting. He'd gone to a lot of trouble to have roses delivered to her this early in the morning. Had her kiss been that good? she thought scathingly. Was this payment for services rendered?

Tempted to crush the card and toss it into the wastepaper basket, she laid it on her desk instead and stared at it as she took a seat in the leather chair. "Thank you for the evening. J." The words implied so much more than there had been. He could make even a courteous gesture seem tawdry.

"Damn him," she cursed under her breath. Unobtrusively, Arlene came in carrying a cup of coffee. Megan barely noticed when it was placed in front of her. She continued to stare at the card and curse the man who had kept sleep at bay all night.

More than she wanted to admit, his kisses and caresses had affected her. Over the past years, while she'd been married to James, and after his death, she'd told herself that the kisses she'd shared with Josh in the gazebo had been embellished by her imagination. That night her emotions had been running high. As a soon-to-be bride, she was feeling loved, desired, beautiful, romantic. No wonder a tall, dark stranger had been able to sweep her off her feet. It was the perfect cliché. But it had only been a fleeting encounter. No big deal.

Why, then, had she never been able to forget it? No,

more than that, why was the memory of it never far from her conscious thought? It lurked on the outskirts of her mind, pouncing out periodically with taunting reminders of her culpability.

"You don't like Josh, do you?" James had asked her one evening over dinner.

Her fork had clattered to her plate. She had laughed nervously. "Of course I like him. What made you ask that!"

"I've hounded you to invite him over for dinner. You've always got an excuse why we can't. Every time he's asked us out, you've found a good reason not to go, but insist that I go alone. It looks to me like you're avoiding him. Why, sweetheart?"

James had been concerned. He had liked the man he worked for. She had teased him about imagining things and promised to have Joshua Bennett over for dinner at the next opportunity—an opportunity that had never come.

At the Bennett Agency office Christmas party, which James begged her to attend with him, Josh's eyes had seemed to follow her like those of a hawk. When he asked her to dance, she was obliged to do so or cause James to wonder at her rudeness. Josh had taken her into his arms with the detachment of an employer dancing with an employee's wife, yet she had sensed the tension in his sleek muscles.

"You look beautiful in Christmas green, Megan," he

had said. Instead of speaking over the music, he spoke under it, intimately.

"Thank you," she murmured, wishing he had changed colognes since the night before her wedding. The fragrance filling her head as he held her within the circle of his deceptively loose arms was far too potent a reminder of how it felt to be pressed firmly against that virile physique.

He had returned her to James the moment the dance ended. As he wished her a Merry Christmas, he kissed her on the cheek. It was a platonic kiss that even the stodgiest spinster couldn't object to. Everyone had laughed, because they were standing under a sprig of mistletoe. But the touch of his warm lips against her skin had robbed Megan of laughter. For some insane reason she had wanted to weep.

And she had. Late that night, lying beside a snoring James, who had celebrated a little too much, she had cried. When they had arrived home, she had seduced him into making love to her. Her uncharacteristic aggression had been desperate and brazen, to the delight of her tipsy husband. Afterward, silently, she had wept bitter tears of remorse. Their lovemaking had never given her the breathless rush of joy, the loss of equilibrium, that Josh's kisses had.

James's embraces left her with a mildly pleasant glow. Josh's sent splinters of feeling missiling through her mind and body, setting off tiny flames that combined into an inferno that wouldn't burn itself out.

Josh had confessed that he'd wanted her in spite of the fact that she was his friend's wife. If she were honest with herself, she'd have to admit that she'd dallied with thoughts of him too. She had loved James, had grieved over his premature death, and missed him still. But always Josh Bennett had stood between them.

There had never been, nor would there ever be, a place for him in her life.

Grimly Megan carried the vase of roses to the credenza under the window. She couldn't ignore them altogether, but she could put them in a less conspicuous place, where she wouldn't have to look at them constantly and thus think about their sender.

The morning passed quickly. Two of her salespeople came in to briefly discuss the peculiarities of specific accounts. Then an advertiser called, irate because, during the evening newscast, his commercial had run for a good ten seconds without audio.

Megan called the production chief, who sheepishly confirmed it. "I'll have to arrange for a make-good, Harry. This is the third one in a month. Don't you realize that every time I have to make good a spot, it costs us a few thousand dollars? Especially if the commercial airs during a newscast."

"Hell, yes, I realize it," he grumbled. "I told you I'm training a new director."

"That's your problem, but I don't think the eleven o'clock news is a good training ground." His muttered curse didn't intimidate her in the least. "Get your act together, Harry."

"It's not fair, you know. You look like an angel, but you've got a heart of stone."

"No one said life was fair." she clicked off the line, only to notice that another call was coming through. Pressing down the blinking lighted button, she said, "What now, Arlene?"

"This isn't Arlene."

For the few hours her mind had been wrapped up in her work, she'd almost forgotten him. Almost. Hearing his voice now, she glanced involuntarily toward the roses. With the sunlight shining on them, the delicate petals were translucent. She couldn't neglect to acknowledge that she'd received them.

"Hello, Josh."

"Hi. How's your day going?"

"Typically. I've been putting out brush fires." His deep chuckle stroked her ear and sent a shiver tiptoeing down her spine. "Thank you for the roses."

"You're welcome."

"I'll return the vase to you as soon—"

"It's yours," he said sharply.

"But—"

"We're reviewing the Seascape commercials this afternoon," he interrupted brusquely. "Terry will be here. He asked that you come over. Ms. Hampson is tied up with another client. He wants your advice on when to air them, etc."

Megan gnawed her bottom lip. "You can advise him on that as well as I can, Josh."

"Yes, but he wants you."

"Then what's he paying you for?" she asked nastily. If it was necessary for her to view the commercials, she would do it gladly, but she had a notion that her being there to voice an opinion was Josh's idea, not Terry's. If Jo Hampson weren't available this afternoon, the preview could be set for another time.

"Do you have an appointment after four o'clock?"

"Yes," she said, without consulting her calendar.

"Four-thirty?" Josh asked tightly. His tone all but said he knew she was lying.

What was the use? She'd have to go. She didn't want another session with Atherton in which she would feel like she'd been tattled on. "Where?" she asked with a weary sigh.

"Here. Ask the receptionist to direct you to the viewing room. As I recall, you've never been here before."

"I wouldn't be coming today if I could help it."

"Four-thirty, Mrs. Lambert," he said briskly, and hung up, his frustration all too apparent.

It couldn't have exceeded hers.

At least she looked coolly professional and not like a flutter-hearted teenager, which was how she felt as she rode up the elevator to the Bennett Agency's suite of offices on the top three floors of the high-rise office building.

Her dress was a crisp linen navy blue with smart brass military buttons down the front and on the patch pockets over each breast. She wore it with navy-and-white spectator pumps. At the time she'd bought the dress, she lamented that she couldn't wear the red blazer that went with it—it clashed with her hair—so she'd settled for one in canary yellow. It might have been second choice, but the combination with her own unique coloring was stunning.

She'd been told how luxurious the offices of the Bennett Agency were, but she wasn't quite prepared for the sight that greeted her when the stainless-steel doors of the elevator whooshed open.

The carpet was dark hunter green and stretched across the expanse to the floor-to-ceiling windows. Couches and easy chairs covered with peach, ivory, or powder-blue damask were scattered strategically throughout the enormous reception area.

"Hello, Ms. Lambert," the receptionist said cordially the moment Megan stepped onto the carpet, which sank a full inch beneath her shoe. "Mr. Bennett and Mr. Bishop are waiting for you. This way, please."

Megan followed her across the room, which was permeated by soft, lilting music coming from invisible speakers. The receptionist, who had the grace, figure, and impeccable grooming of a high-fashion model, opened tall double doors and stood aside to allow

Megan to pass through them. "Thank you," she said before the woman closed the doors quietly behind her.

She hadn't been led to a projection room, but to Josh's office. His desk was gigantic, leather topped, and littered with papers. Storyboards, sketches, scripts, diagrams, magazines, and glossy photographs were strewn across its surface. So his executive image wasn't all for show. He *did* actually work.

"Megan." She turned, startled by his voice. Why did it always sound like a caress? "Forgive us for being so casual, but it's close to quittin' time."

He was coming toward her from a long, deep leather sofa upholstered in chamois-colored kid. He had taken off his suit jacket, as had Terry Bishop, who also stood up to greet her. Josh took her elbow casually and escorted her toward the intimate arrangement of comfortable furniture that might have been found in someone's den.

"Hi, Megan."

"Hello, Terry," she said, extending her hand for him to shake. "It's good to see you again."

"Likewise. When Josh suggested that he invite you to come view the commercials, I thought it was a terrific idea. As I told you last night, I trust your judgment on when to air them—all that stuff I know nothing about."

She cast an accusing glance at Josh, whose golden eyes were dancing with unconcealed mischief. What did he care if he'd been caught in a lie? He'd gotten exactly what he wanted, as always. "We were having a glass of Perrier. Would you like one?" Josh offered.

"No, thank you."

"Juice, coffee, a mixed drink?"

"No," she said with more asperity than necessary. "Thank you," she added for Terry Bishop's benefit.

"Then, let's go into the projection room," Josh said, not in the least perturbed by her hostility.

They made their way through a labyrinth of hallways. Unlike the serenity of the reception area, the corridors of the office complex were like a honeycomb, riddled with chambers of activity and rushing workers.

The projection room contained eight tiered rows of theatre seats. The back wall had a tiny square through which the filmed commercials would be projected onto the large white screen at the front of the room.

"These films will be dubbed onto video-tape cartridges for the television stations' use," Josh said by way of explanation. Seeing her stony expression, he added, "But of course you know that."

"Of course."

Instead of being embarrassed, Josh only grinned and chucked her under the chin. Terry, whose back was turned to take his seat, didn't see the playfully affectionate gesture or the way Megan dodged it.

After a brief conference with the projectionist, Josh sat down in the row behind the one where Megan and Terry sat side by side. She was relieved that Josh hadn't chosen to sit next to her, but her relief was short-lived. As soon as the first commercial began to run, he moved to the edge of his seat and leaned forward to whisper comments.

His forearms were crossed on the backs of their seats. Ostensibly his points were made for the benefit of them both, but his lips were often arousingly close to Megan's ear, her cheek, her neck. His nearness sent tremors throughout her body.

"Well, what do you think?" Terry asked her anxiously when the first sixty-second commercial had run.

He peered at her through thick eyeglasses that magnified his eyes, but she wasn't nearly as aware of them as she was of Josh's amber eyes, capped by a scarred eyebrow, which watched her too closely.

Was Josh looking at her mouth? Nervously, she wet her lips with a darting tongue, then hoped to heaven he didn't think she'd done it to entice him. Terry was waiting for her reply. What had he asked her? "The commercial was beautifully done. The production house you hired did a super job. If all the commercials are this good, within a week of their airing Seascape will be booked up for the year."

Obviously relieved, Terry returned his myopic eyes to the screen, where a couple was walking hand in hand along a deserted beach. They were silhouetted darkly against a vibrant sunrise. Once she looked back at the screen, Megan did a double take. A moment later, she heard Josh's amused drawl.

"No, they're not naked, though they look it, the way they were photographed. We planned it that way, but almost overshot our mark. This commercial borders on being too erotic."

"I hope no one shows up at Seascape expecting a nude beach. We offer a lot of amenities, but that isn't one of them," Terry said, laughing.

Megan couldn't voice a reply. Her eyes were riveted on the man and woman, who were now seen in a close-up silhouetted kiss. Their lips melted together, their bodies gravitating toward each other, until two previously distinct forms became one unbroken shadow. Her heart pounding, Megan realized that the features she projected onto the models were those of herself and—

"I'm sure that, if a couple was so inclined, a private stretch of beach where *no* rules applied could be found." Josh spoke the words secretly into her ear and she closed her eyes to ward off a wave of dizziness.

She had to get out of here. The darkness was too absolute. The curtained walls of the room made her feel claustrophobic. The presence of the man behind her wreaked havoc on her emotional stability.

But there was no escaping. Terry Bishop was already directing another anxiety-ridden question to her about the commercials. How many were there? Five? A dozen? Megan could only hope that they would soon be finished.

They had seen only about half of the commercials

when the receptionist stepped discreetly into the darkened room. "Mr. Bishop? I hate to disturb you, but you have an important call. I've put it through on the telephone in the office across the hallway."

Terry sighed, and stood up. "Thank you," he said to the retreating woman. Megan stood up as well, grateful that she'd been rescued, but it wasn't to be. "No, no, please, Mrs. Lambert. Watch the rest of them. I'll be back as soon as I can."

He inched out of the row of seats and opened the door only wide enough to slip out. The wedge of light decreased with the closing door, until the room was once again plunged into darkness. Megan sat frozen in her chair, afraid to move, afraid to breathe.

In the velvet darkness that surrounded them, she felt Josh move. His arms came around to enclose her. His hands linked across her breasts. "If you had as rough a night as I did, you have no right to look as gorgeous as you do."

When his breath ghosted over her ear that way, she was powerless to move away from it. "I . . . I slept very well."

He caught her lobe in his teeth and worried it tenderly. "You really should do something about this habit you have of lying, Megan. Lord, you taste good." He was taking small bites from the fragile skin behind her ear.

"Josh . . ." What should have sounded like an admonishment came out like an entreaty. What power did he have over her, that he could reduce her to a quivering heap of raw nerves? With him she lost touch with the woman she was to everyone else. Her professionalism flew . . .

Professionalism. Professionalism.

Her mind focused on that word and repeated it like a catechism until it registered. How dare he insult her as a professional by using her as a sexual toy? Reaching up, she threw off his hands from around her neck and vaulted out of the seat. The animated picture showed up watery and diffused on her torso, and a huge shadow of her was cast on the screen.

"You really are a loathsome bastard. Joshua Bennett. How many professional women do you lure into your den under the auspices of business and try to seduce? Well, count me off. I'm above playing footsie with a client."

She picked up her purse from the next seat and made to move out of the aisle, but Josh threw one long leg over the back of her seat and, with an agility that impressed her, jumped over it. He blocked her exit in the narrow aisle.

"This has nothing to do with professionalism, and you damn well know it. I'm not fooled by that excuse, and I don't think you are either. What's between us—"

"There's nothing between us except antipathy and a debt I didn't even know I owed."

"What the hell are you talking about? What debt?"

"You got me my job!" she shouted.

She could tell by his startled expression that he hadn't expected that. "Who told you?" he asked warily.

"Doug Atherton, just yesterday. When I expressed my reluctance to become involved with the Seascape account, he strongly urged that I reconsider. I was then informed of your power play to land me my job."

The expletive that hissed through his angry lips normally would have shocked her, but rage made her immune to such trivialities.

"I never wanted you to know about that."

Her chin jutted out belligerently. "Well, now I do. And I don't know who's been disgraced the most, you for so shamelessly throwing your weight around, or me for unwittingly letting you get away with it. Did you think getting me a job would absolve you from guilt for my husband's death?"

His fingers bit into the tender flesh of her upper arms as he gripped them hard. "I've already told you, James did nothing here that he didn't want to do. As for getting you a job, yes, I wanted to help you out. I would have wanted to help out the widow of any of my employees."

"I didn't want your help! I didn't need it." She shook her head furiously.

"Maybe you didn't, but it didn't hurt you any either."

"You're the last person on earth I would choose to be indebted to."

"You're not indebted to me, damn it," he said through clenched teeth. "I only got you there. You did the rest yourself. I knew you had the talent to carry out the job and to succeed at it. If you were old or ugly, fat or frumpy, I'd have smiled proudly over your accomplishments and at myself for making the right decision and that would have been the end of it."

He moved closer and drew her against his solid body. "That's not the case, though, is it?"

She pleaded with her heart not to knock so solidly against her ribs, for surely he could feel it. *Fight back, Megan.* "It's collection time, is that it?" she demanded. "Why did you wait three years? I'd have thought you wouldn't let a debt ride that long. Am I to thank you for your generosity, or were you just letting the interest, which I'm sure is usurious, accrue? Tell me now, Mr. Bennett, what's the price of my job?"

In the room's dim light his eyes glinted hard and brassy. "I've told you one has nothing to do with the other," he said menacingly. "If you were car-hopping at the local root beer stand, I'd still want you. I don't know what happened to us that night before your wedding, but something did."

"No."

"Yes. Nothing like that has happened to me before or since, and I couldn't have felt as strongly as I did unless you had felt it too. Deny it all you want to, Megan, but you know you're lying—to me and to yourself."

"I felt nothing," she denied hotly, mortified to realize that scalding tears were flooding her eyes.

A stricken expression crossed his face. "Don't cry," he pleaded, crushing her against his chest and stroking her back soothingly. "The last thing I want is to make you cry. I've acted high-handedly. I admit it. But only because I didn't know any other way to get your attention. Please, Megan, don't cry."

His hands cupped her face and tilted it up to his. As the moving picture of a little boy and his father riding a bicycle built for two wavered across their bodies, his lips molded onto hers. His tongue invaded the sweet interior of her mouth even as his body moved suggestively against hers.

Beyond conscious thought, responding purely out of physical and emotional need, she arched against him, fitting her femininity to his complementing masculinity. The contact was exquisite and breathtaking, and their soft gasps of pleasure and pain harmonized. Their hungry mouths refused to be denied as the kiss mellowed to a controlled violence. His arms wrapped around her like bands of steel. Her hands disarranged the soft cloth of his shirt as she scoured the muscles of his back with greedy hands.

They were so lost within their embrace that, when the voice boomed out at them from the overhead speakers, they separated in startled disbelief. Megan stared at Josh with wide, unblinking eyes as her chest heaved like a bellows.

"Will that be all, Mr. Bennett?" the projectionist asked again, apparently unaware of what he'd interrupted.

Megan looked blindly toward the blank screen at the front of the room. The commercials had finished, yet she hadn't viewed one since Terry had left the room. Jolted back into reality, she covered her tingling lips with a shaky hand.

In extreme exasperation, Josh raked his fingers through his hair. "Yes. Thank you, Tad."

The microphone clicked off, and they were left alone in the dark, silent room. "Megan—"

"No," she said shortly, backing away from him. "I don't know what . . . what happens to me when you . . . Consider the debt paid. I think the insults I've suffered from you are more than enough recompense. From now on we're even, Mr. Bennett."

She pivoted on her heels, grabbed up her purse a second time, and groped her way out the aisle to the door. She flung it open, escape uppermost in her mind.

"Megan," Josh shouted from behind her. The name reverberated off the walls of the projection room and was still echoing when she all but collided into a startled Terry Bishop, who was reaching for the doorknob from the other side.

Megan didn't know who was the most dumbfounded. Terry took in her tear-streaked face, her well-kissed swollen lips, the frantic look in her eyes. She followed his gaze to Josh, whose shirttail was half in, half out, his loosened tie lying at a sharp angle on his chest.

"I'm . . . uh . . . excuse me," Terry stuttered apologetically. "That was—was Gayla, my wife. She, uh, wanted me to get your address so she can send you a formal invitation to the grand opening of Seascape, on June first. You're both coming, aren't you?"

Four

M egan could feel how imbecilic the expression on her face was. Absently she reached up to smooth her hair. No doubt the professional respect Terry had for her was disappearing rapidly as she stood there, dully trying to comprehend what he had said and provide some reasonably intelligent response. Her dominant thought was that her escape from Josh had been blocked.

Out of the corner of her eye, she saw Josh nonchalantly tucking in his shirttail and straightening his necktie. He seemed not at all upset by their having been caught like misbehaving children. Had she the ability to control the muscles of her face, her lips would have curled into the frown of contempt she felt inside. Why should his insouciance surprise her? This kind of thing must happen to him all the time.

Indeed, his voice was breezily unaffected when he said, "I wouldn't think of missing the gala opening of the resort, Terry. Thank you."

"It wouldn't be nearly the event it's going to be if we hadn't had your help, Josh," the developer said to him with a respect that nauseated Megan. He turned to her. "Megan, can you make that weekend with us?"

"I—I don't know," she said. If Josh Bennett was going to be there, she certainly wouldn't attend. She'd think up a reasonable excuse later. Now she only wanted to leave. "I'll have to check it out with the station's management. You can send my invitation to the office. Now if you two gentlemen"—she shot a disparaging look in Josh's direction—"will excuse me, I'm meeting another client for dinner." It was another lie, and Josh's arched eyebrow told her he knew it. "Good night," she said, sailing out of the projection room with what modicum of dignity was left her.

She hurried down the hallways, deserted now save for a few diehards—like James had been. *Go home to your wife, your husband, your family. Don't give that man the best of yourself. He's not worth it,* she wanted to shout to them. She raced across the elegant lobby as though escaping a torture chamber.

Later, she didn't even remember the trip home. For once impervious to the traffic, she had driven automatically, her mind cemented on the minutes she had spent alone with Josh. The moment she stepped into her house, she felt the emptiness like a tangible presence, like a shroud blanketing her, smothering her.

"It's his fault that I'm alone," she said aloud in fury and defeat. Were it not for Josh Bennett, she'd still have a husband, maybe even a baby or two by now. She had him to thank for the loneliness in her life. Still he fed on her like a scavenger. When would he consider her picked clean?

He had stolen her husband from her even before his death. James had never belonged to her the way he had belonged to the Bennett Agency. Josh had taken away her dignity by obtaining her job for her. That she'd been unaware of his machinations didn't matter. How many people knew that Josh had secured her job for her? Was she laughed at behind her back? Did everyone think she'd asked for his help? And what did they think she'd done to get it? She shivered as she undressed in the air-conditioned bedroom— but not because she was cold.

Now Josh Bennett was robbing her of self-respect. Each time he touched her, she became like warm, malleable clay molded to his will. Shame washed over her as she recalled how she had arched her body up to his, how her mouth had opened to him.

"I hate him, despise him," she sobbed, gathering her pillow close and bending her knees to her chest in an attitude of self-protection. The pillow blotted salty tears from her cheek.

Don't cry. Megan, don't cry.

"No, no." She protested the memory of his compassionate words. She didn't want to remember the gentleness with which he'd pressed her against him, the tenderness of his hands, the sweetness of his lips. Trying to conjure up an image of a hard, calculating man, she failed. The only picture that came to mind was Josh's concerned expression as he cradled her cheeks and lifted her mouth to his.

"No," she repeated, deeply anguished.

She hated him more than ever, yet only now would she admit to herself the true reason. Since the night they'd met, she had never been able to banish him from her mind. Tenaciously he remained. And he wouldn't be exiled now.

For two days Megan didn't communicate with either Josh or Terry Bishop. She received only a brief report from Jo Hampson. "Terry said you liked the commercials. That poor man's so uptight. If Seascape doesn't open soon, he's going to have heart failure. Thanks for filling in for me the other day."

"Glad to do it," Megan said with what she hoped was a sincere smile. "What kind of schedule did you work out for those convenience-store spots?"

With Seascape momentarily off her hands, she concentrated on wading through the mountain of work that had accumulated on her desk for the past several days. She made overdue telephone calls, answered correspondence, and held a sales meeting for her staff. By the third day, her self-confidence restored, she was feeling a sense of accomplishment. Coming back from a quick yogurt lunch in the basement commissary, her walk was almost jaunty.

Her buoyancy deflated like a punctured balloon

when she opened the door to her office and saw Josh sitting on the couch. Her eyes collided with his, and for an intense moment neither of them moved. Then slowly he unfolded his length from the deep cushions and stood up.

Not only his appearance but also his clothing left her speechless. He was dressed in a black-and-gold sweat suit and running shoes. His hair was windblown, his color high. Had he jogged over?

"Forgive the way I'm dressed."

"What are you doing here?" She closed the door behind her and immediately regretted having done so. To open it now would be an admission that she felt completely undone at having found him here. Stiffly she stood just inside the door, trying vainly not to look at the deep wedge of dark curling hair in the V of the sweat shirt, zipped only halfway up. If that weren't enough, the way the matching pants fit his slim hips was most disconcerting.

"Your secretary was still at lunch," he said, not answering her question. "I decided to wait for you to get back. Do you mind my being here?"

"Does it matter?" she asked acidly.

"Yes." That simple unequivocal statement was more injurious than derision would have been, and she averted her eyes from his as she crossed the room briskly and stowed her purse in a bottom drawer of her desk.

"What can I do for you, Mr. Bennett?" she asked curtly as she assumed her seat.

"You can forgive my behavior the other day." Her eyes flew back to his as her lips rounded into a small O of surprise. "You were right. I took advantage of a business meeting. When I kiss you again, and I will"—his voice lowered significantly—"I promise that the circumstances will be more conducive to romance."

"There won't—"

"Yes, there will be. I'll see to it that there are many such occasions." He looked toward the credenza, where the roses were now opened to their full glory.

Why hadn't she thrown them out? The morning after her encounter with him in the projection room she had closed her hands around the heavy vase with every intention of emptying the blossoms into the large trash receptacle at the end of the hall. But she hadn't been able to bring herself to do so. Why?

Josh walked over and pinched off one of the blossoms, then stepped behind her desk, stopping just inches from her chair. "An olive branch?"

Her heart skidded to a halt, and air felt trapped in her lungs as he extended his hand to her breast. Taking infinite care not to touch her, he slipped the rosebud into the first buttonhole of her blouse. His fingers were slow to withdraw. As they dangled there, a mere inch away, they radiated a longing to caress her so strong that her body responded as if they had indeed touched her. Her breasts swelled with desire, and the nipples tightened and peaked, beckoning to him.

She felt his eyes on the crown of her head. His breathing was rough and labored. Directly in front of her his thighs flexed spasmodically and his stiff fingers closed into fists. She curbed a mad impulse to lift one of those fists, open it, kiss it, and lay it against an aching breast.

"In answer to your question," he said softly, "I've never lured a woman into my place of business for the purpose of seduction. I never mix business with pleasure. You, Megan, are the only woman who ever tempted me to break my own rule. Since I met you, you've been the exception to every rule."

Still she couldn't speak. Why wasn't she casting aspersions on him? She should be lambasting him with every insult her mind could compose.

Instead she sat flustered and mute as he backed slowly away from her and sat down on the sofa once again.

"That's the main reason I wanted to see you today. To apologize. I'm here like this"—he indicated his clothing—"because one of my agents called me while I was at the gym. I thought you should know what he told me right away."

The portentousness in his voice alarmed her. She hadn't heard such grave tones since the day he had called her at home and told her to come to the hospital right away. Her husband was in the emergency room fighting for his life.

"What is it, Josh?" Unconsciously she spoke his name with the intimacy of a valued friend, a . . . lover.

"As you know, one of our major accounts is the Dixieland food-store chain." She nodded. "They're threatening to pull all their advertising off your station and divide it up between your competitors."

"What?" She gasped, knowing immediately the importance of what Josh had told her. Dixieland grocery stores ran television commercials throughout the day and night. Losing their advertising dollars would cause a vacuum in the budget that would be difficult, if not impossible, to fill. *"Why?"*

"Barnes," he said tersely. "Megan, I wouldn't trouble you with this if I thought their complaints were petty. Were this an isolated case, I'd take Dixieland's promotion man to dinner and convince him that pulling their commercials off WONE would be a stupid move. You'd never have to know about it." He stopped suddenly, as if realizing he'd revealed more than he'd intended.

"You've done that before, haven't you?" she demanded, her face paling. "Run interference to protect me?"

"I . . . it—"

"Haven't you?" she asked again, impatiently.

"Yes," he admitted reluctantly. "But that's no more than I do for every sales manager of every television station all over the South. I smooth ruffled feathers all day. That comes with my territory. So don't go all defensive on me, okay? I've done for you what I've done for many others."

Her back was still ramrod-straight and her chin still at a haughty angle, but she said, "Go on."

He studied her for a long time. If she hadn't known him so well, known the kind of man he was, she might have thought his expression was wistful. His eyes scanned her hair, her face, her throat. He looked at the rosebud ensconced between her breasts for long moments. Finally he raised his eyes to hers again, and cleared his throat.

"As I was saying, if this were an isolated case, I'd let it pass. But this is the third time this week I've heard a complaint about WONE. Barnes handles each of those three accounts."

Megan picked up her telephone and punched three numbers. "I need to see you. Now."

She hung up and turned back to Josh. "Thank you for telling me. I can take care of it from here."

"I'd like to stay."

"I'd rather you didn't."

"I'll stay."

Before she could offer another argument, Barnes was opening her door, looking very uncomfortable. "Come in." She was upset with Barnes, but not near-ly as much as she was with Josh. One minute he was presenting her with rosebuds and whispering humble apologies; the next he was interfering in her life with the cold insensitivity she had come to expect from him.

Barnes sidled inside and closed the door behind him. He blanched visibly and wiped his palms down the sides of his pants legs when he glanced at Josh lounging on the couch. He didn't even seem to notice Josh's casual attire. "Mr. Bennett." He nodded respectfully.

His genuflection to Josh only heightened Megan's irritation. "All right, Barnes, let's hear it. There had better be a damn good excuse why three of Mr. Bennett's clients have complained about you this week."

"Three?" he squeaked.

"Three or one, it doesn't matter," Megan said, her aggravation showing. "I gave you fair warning at the beginning of the week that you'd better shape up. Now the principal of the largest advertising agency in this part of the country comes to me, in an emergency situation, to tell me we may lose one of our largest accounts, and all because of your ineptitude."

Ignoring Barnes's stammering attempt to defend himself, she swung her fiery gaze to Josh. "Mr. Bennett, would you, for my sake as well as Barnes's, enumerate the complaints you've heard?"

With the sober intonation of a judge, Josh ticked off the incriminating derelictions of duty—misrepresentation of when the client's commercials would run, misquotation of the rates, blatant indifference, total lack of communication. With each transgression cited, Barnes's face collapsed further, until he had the countenance of the saddest of basset hounds.

When Josh was finished, he swung his eyes from a distraught Barnes to Megan. "Thank you, Mr. Bennett, for warning us of this. Let's hope there's time to make amends. Any comments, Barnes?"

The young man shook his head miserably. "I've been messing up. I know it."

"Well, if you want pity, you've come to the wrong place. If you want that girl in the newsroom, then go after her and go after her to win her, or give her up, or find a substitute for her, or take cold showers. I don't care."

Barnes stared, stupefied, at Megan, clearly surprised to learn that she knew the source of his problem. As a woman she wanted to confess that she knew exactly what it was like to let someone consume one's thoughts and override one's common sense. But as an executive she couldn't afford to give an inch.

"I'm not going to divide your account list among the other salesmen, because they all have heavy loads. Nor am I going to threaten to replace the good ones you have with those that are less desirable. I don't think you'd care. What I am going to do is put you on one month's probation. For my part, that's a generous amount of time. At its termination I'm going to call personally on all your accounts. If they aren't completely satisfied and singing your praises, you might just as well clear out your desk, because you'll be gone by that working day." She consulted her calendar. "That will be June twelfth. Have I made myself clear?"

He nodded glumly. "Yes, Meg—, uh, Ms., uh . . . ma'am."

"Thank you for responding so promptly to my summons," she said by way of dismissal. Barnes dragged himself to the door and closed it behind him.

Megan rose from her chair, feeling the weight of responsibility on her shoulders. She went to the window and stared out at a gorgeous spring day. Her eyes closed against the bright sunlight, which she dimmed by closing the blinds a notch. The sounds of traffic on the downtown streets were muted. She felt Josh's hands on her shoulders before she knew he was standing behind her.

"So a woman is his problem," he said softly as his hands massaged the tension from her neck and shoulders. Through the thin fabric of her blouse, his hands were warmly comforting.

"Yes. Maybe I shouldn't have chastised him in front of you, but I thought your presence might increase the urgency of what I was telling him, shame him into doing what I know he's capable of doing. I don't know whether I handled it the right way or not." It felt so good to confide her uncertainty to him.

"You handled it just great."

"Do you think so, Josh?" She didn't examine why his opinion meant so much to her.

He turned her around to face him. "You were wonderful, brilliant," he whispered, smoothing one hand down her hair while the other propped up her chin. "If I were young Barnes, I'd get my tail in gear and try to get on your better side."

She smiled skeptically back at him. "That remains to be seen."

"I'm so damn proud of you. I knew you were tough. I'd heard reports that you were sharper than a tack. But I didn't expect you to be quite so terrific."

"The occasion called for being tough. I had to shake him up."

"That's what makes you a good sales manager."

"But at the same time I hated to come down on him so hard."

"That's what makes you a woman."

She had almost convinced herself that she wore an armor of anger to protect herself from him, but his softly spoken words pierced right through it like the cleanest stroke of a rapier and plunged straight into her heart. Headlong she dived into the depths of the eyes that looked down at her, and she begged to be drowned in them. His hands slid down her arms to clasp her hands. With no other part of their bodies touching, he leaned forward and sealed her mouth with his.

The sweet taste of his lips and the slow, evocative

marauding of his tongue inside her mouth held her captive as strong arms couldn't have. At some silently given command, their heads rotated and switched sides to enjoy each other further. He sipped at her lips deliciously before pulling slightly away.

"Have dinner with me."

"I—"

He kissed her again, drawing her breath into his own body.

"Please. Dinner only, Megan. I swear it. Just let me be with you."

"Josh," she whispered. This was insanity, and she well knew it, but she couldn't resist his seductive kisses. Her will, her reason, her grim resolutions scattered like petals in the wind whenever he touched her. She recognized now, if never before, that she feared what became of her when she was with Joshua Bennett. Could she be held accountable for mistakes made when he robbed her of the ability to think?

"Dinner and dancing. Nothing else, if you say so."

Would one night hurt? One harmless dinner? A little dancing? He tasted so good. Salty. He'd had time for some form of exercise before receiving the call at the gym and coming to her. The musky smell of him made her light-headed. She longed to touch the coarse mat of hair on his chest, to trace its origins just below his collarbone, to chart the pattern of its growth down his torso, coming eventually to the root of his masculinity. She swallowed with difficulty.

"Please, Megan, end this punishment. Say yes." He pressed his lips sweetly against hers and caressed them lovingly.

"Oh, Josh, ye—"

They heard the shuffling footsteps a split second before there was a sharp tap on the door and it was pushed open. "Megan?"

They sprang apart as Doug Atherton and Terry Bishop entered.

"There are you," Doug said heartily. "Your secretary's not back from lunch yet, and I couldn't find you anywhere else in the building." He seemed not to notice Megan's stricken expression. "I called your office, Josh. They said you were coming here. Did you jog over?" He laughed.

"No," Josh said. "Something urgent came up that I thought Megan should know about. I rushed over before my workout was finished."

"Nothing critical, I hope." Atherton's brow wrinkled with instant alertness.

"No, I don't think so," Josh said easily. "Megan managed to iron it out."

"Ah, good, good. Nice flowers," he added offhandedly, indicating the vase of roses. "Megan, Terry told me you'd seen the commercials, but he wanted to talk to you about them."

The man had barely looked at her. He was too smart not to put two and two together, after having caught her and Josh alone twice in recent days. Both times they'd looked startled and guilty. "Hi, Terry," she said cordially for Doug's benefit. "Let's all sit down, shall we?"

She returned to her desk, grateful that she could place it between her and the three men. Suddenly she felt vulnerable and defenseless. "What can I do for you, Terry?"

"Well," he said, wetting his lips nervously, "I was worried about the placement of the commercials. You know, about which one should air when. Do you have any ideas along that line?"

She felt a moment of panic. How many of them had she seen? Two? three? She didn't remember any that had run after Terry left the room. The only one that had left a lasting impression was the one with the couple in silhouette. Remembering it now, she grew excessively warm and glanced at Josh. The agate eyes watching her closely told her he knew all too well what she was thinking. She'd have to fake her way through this.

"Well, I think the one with the couple on the beach should air late at night," she quipped. Her ploy worked. Terry and Josh laughed. After a hasty explanation from Josh, Doug joined them.

"As for the others, let's see." She pursed her lips as though trying to remember, praying that something would come to her blank mind.

"Megan and I talked this over while you were on the telephone, Terry," Josh said. Her eyes widened in surprise at his lie, but fortunately he held the attention of the other two men and they didn't notice her dismay. "She and I both feel that the commercials relating to the shopping areas and the other amenities appealing to women should run during the daytime, when the lady of the house is watching soap operas or quiz shows."

"Exactly," Megan said quickly, wanting to contribute something and not appear the idiot she felt herself to be.

"The commercials showing the golf courses, tennis courts, and fishing charters, should run in the evening, when the man of the house is at home, and during televised sports events. As for the ones showing the children on bicycles and romping on the beach, the choice is clear—afternoons and Saturday mornings. Isn't that what we decided, Megan?"

"Y-yes, absolutely," she said. Her hands were locked together tightly on her desk top. She hoped no one noticed her white knuckles. "That way a particular commercial reaches the audience that would have the most interest in it." The words were trite, even lame, but better than nothing. Was Doug eyeing her strangely? Terry, at least, seemed pleased.

"Well," he said, slapping his thighs and standing up, "you've reassured me once again. I'm sorry to have taken up your time. When do the commercials begin airing?"

"Tomorrow," Megan answered promptly, grateful

that she and Jo had discussed the starting schedule only that morning.

Terry reached across her desk to shake her hand. "Then I probably won't be seeing you until the opening on Hilton Head."

"But . . . I won't be able to attend. I'm sorry, but—"

"She'll be there, Terry," Doug said expansively. He turned to where she stood behind the false security of her desk. "Josh called me this morning. He told me about your reluctance to go to Hilton Head for the opening of Seascape because of your work load here. Much as we like having you around," he said like an affectionate, indulgent parent, "I think we can spare you for a few days."

The seconds ticked by while she stared slack-jawed at Doug. Then she turned to glare at Josh. "Mr. Bennett called on *my* behalf?" She tried to keep her voice coquettish and light, but she felt like snarling.

Doug chuckled. "Yes. He lit into me good and proper because I wasn't letting you go. I finally convinced him that I didn't even know about the grand-opening festivities and that, of course, you'd go."

She swallowed the hot anger that threatened to choke her. "Isn't it usually the national sales manager's privilege to attend functions if they relate to accounts out of the state?" she asked with a sweet innocence that was contrary to the rage boiling inside her.

"Yes, but he's going to be in New York that first week of June for an NBA convention." He turned to Terry. "National Broadcasters Association." The developer nodded. "Anyway, he's not nearly as familiar with this account as you are."

"Then you should go." She hoped the desperation in her voice would be taken for enthusiastic generosity.

"Wish I could, wish I could, but I'm working on that deal in Savannah to buy that radio station. You go and have a good time. Right, Terry? You're not asking her in order to make her work all the time she's there, are you?"

"Of course not," Terry replied hastily. "We want everyone to have a good time."

"Then, it's settled," Doug said with satisfaction, patting his rounded belly. "Terry's invited you to fly on his corporate jet. Josh can fill you in on the specifics. Ready, Terry?" Without waiting for an answer, Doug opened the door. Terry followed. "Josh?" Doug queried as he held the door for him.

"Not just yet. Megan and I still have some items to discuss."

"See you both later, then."

Her boss bustled out, and Megan was left alone with the man who was chiseling away at the foundation of her life. No sooner had the door clicked shut than she rounded on him.

Raising both palms placatingly, he said quickly, "It's not what you think."

"The hell it's not," she snapped.

"Left on your own, you would have declined the invitation."

"Damn right."

"I wasn't going to stand idly by and see that happen."

"What business is it of yours?" she shouted.

"*You* are my business, damn it. I made you my business the first night I saw you."

Seething, she stepped around the corner of her desk and paced between it and the door. "For three years you left me in blessed peace. Now, in one week's time, you've bulldozed your way into my life, manipulating it, manipulating me. Why? Why now? Why not as soon as James's body was cold?"

He cursed under his breath. "For three years I let you stew in your own bitter juices. Do you think I'm stupid? I knew you didn't want to be seen, touched, or spoken to by me. When I saw this chance with Seascape as a means of getting to you, then, by God, yes, I took it. I doubt it you'd have accepted a date with me if I'd called you up and simply asked as any decent guy would."

"Right again!"

"So," he continued as though she hadn't spoken, "I used whatever devices I could. Manipulation, you say? All right, yes. But what choices did you leave me?"

"No choices! You weren't entitled to any. You should have taken my hints and given up entirely. The message was, *is,* clear. I don't want anything to do with you, Joshua Bennett. Once and for all, let that sink in and leave me alone."

His features softened considerably, and a rueful half-smile tugged at the corner of his mouth. "I can't, and you know why."

She faced him like an adversary, her breasts expanding with emotion and heat, her cheeks hot from feelings she didn't want to acknowledge.

"Why did you bother with a poetic invitation to dinner?" she asked haughtily. "You already knew Doug would see to it that I went to Hilton Head."

He spread his arms wide on either side of his body. "You see! That's what I'm talking about. I try to go about seeing you in the conventional way, and you find fault with that too." He let his arms fall to slap loudly against his thighs.

"Megan," he said with shriveling patience. "We need that weekend together. Away from this." He indicated the office with a wave of his hand. "Away from the past. Away from James's ghost." He stepped closer to her. "We need time to learn about each other, to laugh, love." His voice had lowered to a husky whisper that entranced her. "I put pressure on Doug this morning because I want you on that island. With me."

Even as she struggled to shut out his words, they thrilled her. Her heart threatened to surrender unconditionally. In one last desperate effort, she gathered her wits and marched to the office door, pulling it open. "Well, thanks to your sneaky blackmailing, I'll be on that cursed island, but not with you, Joshua Bennett."

He sauntered toward her and, before she could deflect him, captured and held her jaw, tilting her head back. "You're absolutely irresistible when you're mad. Your hair fairly crackles, like fire. And I love the way my full name looks and sounds on your lips."

She thought he was going to kiss her, but he didn't. Instead he stared at her mouth for a long time.

"We're not on the island yet, Megan. Don't make any vows you won't be able to keep," he warned her. His thumb made a sensuous trail across her lips before he dropped his hand. He brushed past her to the outer office. He'd closed the far door behind him before she noticed a wide-eyed Arlene staring up at her, her hands frozen over her typewriter.

"You wouldn't want to be on an island with *him*?" she asked in round-eyed disbelief.

"If you think he's so great, why don't *you* go with him to Hilton Head?"

"He didn't ask *me*."

"Ohhh!" Megan ground out and, turning on her heel, slammed back into what had been the sanctuary of her office. She yanked the rosebud out of her buttonhole and crushed it between her fingers, filtering the fragrant remnants into the trash can. "He didn't ask *me*," she mimicked her secretary.

Lord, what did women see in the man? He was rude, overbearing, arrogant, and completely without scruples. What other man would kiss his friend's fiancée the night before the wedding?

Yet women adored him. His romantic involvements were legion. He discarded women heartlessly and went on to others and still they were drawn to him like steel shavings to a magnet. His flamboyant romances were often in the headlines of the society pages. The headlines . . .

Headlines!

What could she do to Josh Bennett that would hurt him the most? Malign his advertising agency? No. It was too reputable. Besides, she couldn't do that without hurting her own business. What would bring public ridicule on a man who had an overabundance of self-confidence? What would be a fitting comeuppance for what he had done to her and James?

She crowed with glee as a plan began to evolve in her mind. Terry Bishop had said media reps would be crawling all over Seascape. Megan Lambert was a nobody, but Josh Bennett wasn't. He'd be noticed. His activities would be chronicled. His new "love" interest would be played up. "Romance Abounds in New H.H. Resort." Her eyes danced with malicious glee as she envisioned the headlines.

Rushing to her desk, she consulted her calendar. "Two weeks," she mused aloud. She had two weeks to prepare herself, to buy all the bait she'd need to set a seductive trap.

When she got on that corporate airplane, Josh Bennett wouldn't recognize the purring woman beside him as the same one who had spat nails at him today.

Five

The chic white pants suit gave Megan the confidence she needed to push through the glass door of the private airfield's terminal. She knew how well the slacks fit her compact figure, how the rounded contours of her derriere were defined by their snugness. The jacket, styled like that worn by baseball players, went over a silk shell in bold stripes of green, yellow, and blue. The silk clung to breasts, which were only partially confined by a wispy, lacy bra, the likes of which Megan had never worn before. Like all the garments she had purchased in the past two weeks, she had chosen it to inspire masculine interest.

The rubber soles of her casual shoes made no noise as she walked the length of the deserted hallway. Over one shoulder she carried the two pieces of luggage that matched the lime-colored stripe in her blouse. Bought with her new wardrobe, the soft, zippered travel bags defied the conservatism that would have usually governed her selections. On her other arm she carried a huge white straw bag.

"Mrs. Lambert?" An attendant rushed toward her. She turned to acknowledge him.

"Yes?"

The uniformed man smiled congenially. "You're the last of Mr. Bishop's party to arrive."

"Oh, I hope I haven't kept them waiting."

"No," he said quickly. "The plane is still being serviced. Everyone is waiting in the main lobby. Allow me," he said, reaching for her bags.

About to hand them over to him, she hurriedly changed her mind. "Thank you, but I think I'll hang on to them for a while."

"Okay. This way."

He indicated the end of the hallway, which Megan could see opened into a large waiting area, where she knew Josh would be. She drew in a deep, shuddering breath. Could she pull this off? Would he fall for her ploy? For all she knew, he could have given up on her and invited another woman to go with him to Hilton Head. They hadn't communicated since he had left her office with that challenge ringing in her ears: *"We're not on the island yet, Megan. Don't make any vows you won't be able to keep."*

She recalled that taunt now as she squared her shoulders and entered the wide lobby. He was pacing back and forth in front of the plate-glass window overlooking the runway, looking like an expectant father.

The moment he saw her, the tension in his face relaxed into a broad smile, and he came striding toward her. His casual tan slacks were too well tailored not to call attention to the length and muscular perfection of his legs. Nor could anyone be impervious to the breadth and strength of his chest and shoulders beneath the soft yellow polo shirt. The sunglasses perched atop his head mussed his hair and gave him a rakish aspect, as did the crooked eyebrow, which arched now as he smiled winningly.

"Hello, Megan." The nervous gladness in his greeting, which came out in a rush, made him sound relieved. Hadn't he been expecting her?

She smiled, convincing herself that the sudden pounding of her heart was due, not to his speaking her name in that invariably intimate way, but to her nervousness over the plan that she must now enact. "Hi, Josh." Her lashes curtained her eyes only briefly before she lifted them in what she hoped was a flirtatious manner.

If his penetrating stare was any indication, he was captivated, if not stunned, by her uncharacteristic warmth. "How have you been?" he asked.

"Well. You?" she replied, looking openly into the eyes that poured like golden honey over her upturned face.

"Busy. Bishop's like a kid going off to kindergarten. For my sake as well as his, I'll be glad when Seascape is in full swing."

His mouth tilted up in a roguish way, and Megan's fingertips tingled with an urge to touch his lips. Her lashes fluttered again, this time involuntarily. "Th-thank you for the Stewart account. Mr. Stewart told me you had highly recommended us on the grounds of our high ratings."

"You're welcome, but I was only being honest. The ratings taken in May show that your eleven-o'clock newscast is now number one in the market. Stewart's advertising dollar couldn't be spent in a better place."

This conversation was meaningless, and they both knew it. Megan could barely keep her eyes off him, while his were transmitting messages that pumped adrenaline through her body. To get back on track, she winced and shifted the straps of her luggage to a more comfortable position.

"Here." He responded immediately, and she couldn't help but be impressed by his manners. "I'm sorry. Let me take that." He reached to relieve her of the luggage, slipping the strap down her arm. Was it her imagination or did his fingers graze the side of her breast? If not, why had her nipples sprung to life beneath their lacy confinement?

"Thank you," she said, smiling up at him tremulously. Some women might enjoy simpering like witless fools, but to her it was demeaning. She didn't want to be coddled, did she?

"Bishop has provided cold drinks, wine or beer for us. Would you like something?"

"No, thank you . . . Josh."

Tearing her eyes from his, she glanced at the cluster

of people waiting for the airplane to take off. She recognized representatives from television stations as well as executives from the business and banking worlds and journalists from major newspapers. Among them were several attractive women, including Laura Wray, travel editor for the *Atlanta Constitution*.

Megan didn't think Josh was escorting one of these women. He had been alone when she arrived. Still, she needed to put that one worry to rest. She wet her lips nervously and was taken slightly aback to see the sudden flare of interest in Josh's eyes. "Are you . . . I mean . . . is anyone . . . with you?"

Again his lips lifted into a grin. He glanced over his shoulder, and the travel editor raised her wineglass in a silent salute. Josh nodded in acknowledgment and turned back to Megan, his smile wider. "No," he said. "That is, not until now."

Letting jealousy have its way, Megan narrowed her gaze speculatively as she assessed the tall, willowy newspaper columnist. "Ms. Wray seems more than a little attentive where you're concerned." Had she ever heard their names linked together? There had been so many, she couldn't remember if Laura Wray was among Josh's stable of women. "Are you sure she hasn't made plans for you once we get to Hilton Head?" she asked, cocking her head to one side, a gesture that she knew arched her throat attractively.

"She may very well have made plans, but she didn't consult me. And unless her plans are that you and I spend a great deal of time alone together, they don't coincide with mine." He took a step closer, until she had to lift her chin a notch higher to look up at him. "I'm glad you came, Megan," he said with soft urgency.

For a moment high emotion prevented her from speaking. "Are you?"

"Yes. More than you can imagine."

"I'm glad I came, too."

"Up until the last minute I was afraid you wouldn't. I wanted to call every day but was afraid I'd only pester you into not coming. It's been hell to stay away from you for two weeks, but I thought you needed that time to think about what this trip could mean to us."

"I wouldn't have missed it." The intensity with which he looked at her mouth made her motivations for going to Hilton Head nebulous and her thinking unclear. What should have been indelibly imprinted on her brain became blurred. Josh always had that effect on her.

"I think they're ready for us to board," he said, breaking into her turbulent thoughts. "Come on. Let's get a good seat."

He hoisted her bags onto his shoulder and, placing his hand in the middle of her back, propelled her toward the tarmac, where the corporate jet whirred in readiness.

Only a few of the other guests had preceded them to the steps going into the airplane. As Megan walked ahead of him, she felt Josh's hand slide from her back to her waist and then for an instant to the curve of her hip. She credited her momentary vertigo to rebellion over his familiar gesture.

Once inside the aircraft, she scanned the seats available. Laura Wray was already settled in one row of seats near the front. "Hello, Josh," she said in a low drawl.

"Laura," he said from behind Megan. "It's nice to see you. Do you know Mrs. Lambert?"

Appraising, but not hostile, blue eyes slid to Megan. "Mrs. Lambert. Laura Wray, *Atlanta Constitution.*"

Megan shook the slender hand extended to her. "Megan, please. I'm with WONE."

"You're not on the air?"

"No, I'm local sales manager."

"It's a pleasure to meet you."

It was difficult to determine the nature of the woman's smile, but Megan categorized it somewhere between sad and wistful.

"I don't think those seats across the aisle are taken," she said. Again Megan noted a hopefulness in her throaty voice.

"No," Josh said, vetoing the idea before Megan could voice an opinion. "The sun will be on that side once we take off. I've already sighted some seats back here." Gently but firmly he pushed Megan along the narrow aisle. "See you later, Laura," he said dismissively.

"Yes. See you later." Her voice trailed off.

Megan sat in the window seat Josh indicated. He placed her bags in a tiny closet at the rear of the plane, then came back to sit beside her. "Comfortable?"

"Yes, but I can't get the seat belt out. It's wedged between the seat and the wall."

He leaned over her to examine the problem. "I think I can." Reaching across her lap, he grasped the nylon strap and tugged hard. His elbow bumped into her breast, not painfully, but with enough vigor to freeze them both for stunned seconds.

His eyes swept down to survey any damage. "I'm sorry," he said gruffly, staring at her breasts. "Did I hurt you?"

Not trusting herself to answer, she only shook her head. With another, more careful tug, the strap came free and Josh buckled it around her, taking an inordinate amount of time adjusting its length. His hands lingered unnecessarily on her abdomen after the metal had already clicked shut. He adjusted his own seat belt with far less ceremony.

As Terry Bishop's other invited guests took their seats, they stopped to speak to Megan and Josh. Those she didn't already know, he introduced her to. She saw the envy in the eyes of the women and knowing speculation in those of the men.

It rankled that everyone automatically assumed she was Josh's latest conquest and traveling companion, but that was the price she was going to have to pay for victory. If all went according to her plan, by the end of the weekend, portable typewriters and telephone wires back to Atlanta would be humming with the news that the local sales manager of WONE and Josh Bennett were an "item." That her late husband had been Josh's employee would only make the story juicier.

"How's Barnes?" Josh asked her over the purr of the jet engines once they were airborne.

She turned to him slightly, and when her knee nudged against his in the narrow space, she allowed it to rest there. "Maybe I should be asking you. Have you had any more complaints?"

"Not even a whiff of one. I think you scared the hell out of him." His teeth were a startling white against his tanned, ruggedly handsome face. The sun on Hilton Head's beach would only enhance the richly bronzed color of his skin.

"I'm keeping close tabs on him," Megan said. "The parent-company bigwigs were down this week. They've increased my budget. I can't afford any costly mistakes. But besides that, I'd hate to let Barnes go. He's a super salesman when he applies himself."

"You're rare, Megan." The intimate pitch of Josh's voice brought her eyes up to his. "You combine professionalism with pure femininity."

The tightening muscles in her throat made talking difficult, but she said, "That's not so rare these days. Many women serve in the capacities usually reserved for men and do admirably well."

He considered the idea for a moment, then said, "Yes, but many women would love to cut a man down to size just for the hell of it, to justify her holding that position, to elevate her own ego. You, on the other hand," he said, leaning nearer, "didn't enjoy it. You hated lighting into poor Barnes. That's the difference I was talking about. Even though you hold what is typically a man's job, make executive decisions daily, you never for one moment forget that you're a woman." He was precariously close now. "Nor does anyone else."

Josh's words made her stiffen with guilt. Wasn't she secretly planning to do exactly what he'd just praised her for *not* doing—cutting a man down to size just to elevate her own ego? Where once revenge had seemed so sweet, it now tasted foul in her mouth. Was there any honor in cutting a man down and reveling in doing it? Her motives were justifiable, but would other people see her as a grasping, clawing, vicious female who'd been scorned?

She felt the need to defend herself. "That's why I must constantly be on my guard, to make sure that no one takes advantage of me because of my sex." He couldn't misinterpret the accusation in her voice.

"I've never taken advantage of that, Megan."

"Haven't you?"

"I've used my position in the advertising field to benefit you. Granted, I wanted you to come on this trip for selfish reasons, but I also thought you needed a break from office pressures. To my knowledge I've never done anything that was detrimental or harmful to you, as a woman or as a professional."

"That's a matter of opinion, isn't it?" Her tone was stinging.

"Name one time I did something to hurt you. I'm ignorant of it."

She opened her mouth, but no words came. What could she blame him for? That she held a prestigious, well-paying job because of his intervention? That WONE never wanted for new advertisers because he directed them to her? That only two weeks ago he had prevented disaster by enlightening her on the Dixieland food-store chain's intentions? What crime could she hang him for?

The original one.

"You kissed me the night before I was to marry your friend."

"A lot of men kissed you that night."

"Not like you did!" she retorted in a harsh whisper.

His eyebrows shot up. "So you're finally admitting that my kiss affected you differently from any other?"

"No!"

"Liar."

By now her agitation was plain. She breathed in quick, rapid pants that stirred the silk over her breasts. She clenched her hands to keep them from slapping him, or caressing him, or from covering the puckering crests of her breasts. She whipped her head around to stare out the window.

Employing feminine wiles had never been necessary for her to attract men. She'd always had plenty of dates, yet she'd gone to her marriage bed a virgin. Except for those tumultuous minutes in the gazebo with Josh, she was innocent of sexual indiscretion. She didn't know how one went about such things, and now she would be feeling her way along with each step. But she did know a woman didn't bring a man to a lathered, heated, leash-straining state by bristling at him every time he became intimate.

She allowed her features to mellow before facing him again. "I'm sorry, Josh." She saw his hand, only inches from hers on the armrest and, swallowing the last of her pride and hesitation, covered it with her own. "I don't want to fight with you any more."

His hand turned over and gripped hers tightly. "Damn it, I wish you'd chosen a less public place to tell me that," he rasped.

"Why?" She raised inquiring eyes to his, and her breath was choking off when she saw desire like hot coals smoldering in his gaze. The gold flecks leaped and danced like tongues of flames.

"I want to kiss you, that's why. I want to celebrate the fact that you no longer see me as a monster, at best the enemy. I've waited three years to hear you say the fight between us is over."

He squeezed her hand tighter. "Megan, did you think I was proud of what I did that night? I didn't walk into that party planning to sweep James's bride into my arms, kiss her as I did, and wish to God she were mine instead of his." He shook his head, and the sunglasses became dislodged. He took them off and stared at his own reflection in the lenses as he continued. "I've done a lot of things I'm ashamed of, but please believe me when I say the last thing I wanted was to make you unhappy or guilty by kissing you."

"I was. The next night when I went to bed with James, I felt very guilty. And for a long time after that."

"I know," he said on a long sigh. "I would have wished only joy for you, yet it seems as if, since I first met you, I've brought you nothing but grief. But then"—his eyes bore into hers—"I could no more have stopped myself from kissing you that night than I could have stopped myself from breathing and gone on living. It was something I *had* to do." Her lips quivered at his words. "Lord, I want to hold you right now."

She lowered her eyes and squeezed them shut in an effort to stabilize senses that had gone haywire. Her world had slipped off its axis and was spinning chaotically in a universe of conflicting emotions.

"Are you too warm? Do you want to take off your jacket?" he asked, seemingly out of context.

Looking back up at him, she shook her head. "No. Why?"

His mouth came down to within scant inches of her ear. "Because I want to see why the stripes on your blouse dip and swell so beguilingly." His voice dropped another decibel. "I want to look at your breasts and fantasize about the way they look and feel."

The warm color that flooded her cheeks couldn't have been faked, and she stared at him speechlessly. After a brief trip into eternity, she regained the use of her vocal cords. "Then, I think it would be best if I left my jacket on."

He sighed, smiling ruefully. "Considering the social restrictions of our surroundings, perhaps it would."

But he continued to hold her hand. Even when several other passengers converged on them for a clamorous discussion of the long weekend ahead, he didn't release it. She looked down at their two hands clasped together on the armrest. His was dusted with dark hair, hers smooth. His was long and strong, hers frail by comparison. His connoted protectiveness; hers looked in need of protection. For the life of her, she couldn't think of a good reason to withdraw her hand from his.

Their descent and disembarkation were carried off without a hitch. A line of limousines waited in front of the Hilton Head Airport to whisk away Seascape's invited guests, who would be arriving throughout the day. Terry was there to greet them personally.

After shaking hands with Josh, he pecked Megan's cheek. "I want you to meet my wife," he said hastily, and it was all Megan could do to keep from laughing at his anxious but endearing manner. Josh, too, if his cocked eyebrow was any indication, was constraining his laughter. Terry designated a limousine for them and said, "I'll ride with you, if that's all right," before turning to greet another guest.

Josh handed the driver Megan's bags as well as his own, which he had picked up as they were shuttled from the plane to the terminal. No sooner had he ducked into the back seat, where she was already seated, than he took her in his arms and pulled her against him.

"Josh—" was the only startled word allowed past her lips before he trapped them with his mouth. His lips opened over hers in a kiss as erotic, as thorough, and as mind-stealing as its predecessors. Megan wasn't even aware of the driver's closing the trunk of the car and assuming his place behind the steering wheel. She couldn't think past the splendor of being held firmly against Josh's body or the exquisite texture of his tongue as it rubbed against hers in a mating rhythm.

Only when she heard Terry's shoes tapping on the concrete sidewalk did she murmur a protest. Josh, too, must have been aware that they were soon to have company. He pulled away, only to kiss her hard and quick again, saying under his breath, "There's a smudge of lipstick on your chin."

She was still blotting at it when Terry opened the door and moved in beside her. "Whew, what a day."

As the car glided through the avenues of the recently developed island, he recounted everything that had happened since he'd last seen them.

"Have you been to Hilton Head before, Megan?" he asked excitedly. She could see his pride not only in his own resort, but also in the beautiful island itself.

"Yes, once my—" She looked swiftly at Josh. "My husband, James, and I came here for a long weekend. I loved it." She glanced through the tinted windows at the deep forest that had been saved from destruction. "I love the South in general, with its moss-draped live oaks and pine trees. I also love the coast and beach. Hilton Head is the one place I've seen that combines both."

"Well put," Josh exclaimed. If her mentioning James had bothered him, he didn't show it. "Maybe I should hire you to write copy for commercials and print ads." They all laughed.

"The original developers were unique, in that they wanted to preserve as much of the natural flavor of the island as possible," Terry explained. "Did you know that at one time a huge cotton plantation stood on the island, even before it became a game preserve?"

"Yes. And wasn't there a significant Civil War battle fought here?" Megan asked.

Terry glanced at Josh and winked. "She's not only pretty, Josh, she's smart, too."

Josh's leonine eyes scanned her face possessively, proudly. "I noticed that a long time ago."

Only the sight of the impressive gates as they

entered Seascape could have unlocked her gaze from his. Flanked by beds of flowers blooming in profusion, the raw-wood entrance branded with the distinctive yet unobtrusive logo for Seascape led into a lane bordered with live oaks dripping with moss. Their massive branches made a shady canopy over the narrow road.

"Oh, Terry," Megan exclaimed, but it was Josh's thigh her hand found and squeezed hard in her excitement. "It's like something out of *Gone With the Wind*."

Terry beamed, evidently pleased with her delight. On either side of the road behind the trees stretched acres of emerald golf greens. Bridle paths ribboned the otherwise untouched woods beyond. Megan felt overwhelmed, trying to take it all in. Seascape's main building was another delightful surprise. The sprawling complex was built almost exclusively of glass and wood, and it blended harmoniously with is woodland setting.

"It's wonderful, Terry," she said, stepping out of the limousine, which had come to a stop in front of wide glass doors. "Absolutely perfect. I don't know what I expected, but this surpasses it."

"Come inside."

Well-trained bellmen, athletic men for the most part, scurried to get people checked into their bungalows with the least inconvenience. Most guests were conveyed to their cottages in golf carts.

"I've already assigned you to a building, so I'll just

get the keys and send you on your way," Terry said hospitably.

Megan nodded absently. She was gaping at the lobby like a country bumpkin in the city for the first time. What impressed her most was that none of the decor was gaudy or inhibiting. Even amidst the luxury, she sensed a homey, comfortable atmosphere.

"Look, Josh." Unthinkingly she took his hand and turned him in the direction of an indoor waterfall, which tumbled over carefully arranged railroad ties and natural stone into a sparkling fountain. Flowers of every species and color surrounded it like a blooming picture frame.

He put an arm around her shoulders and drew her close to his side. "Glad you came?" he asked into her hair.

Forgetting all about her devious plans, past heartaches, and hopes for retribution, she looked up at him with undisguised pleasure and answered honestly, "Yes."

"This is Greg," Terry said from behind them. They turned to face a college-aged young man with American good looks who was smiling in a friendly fashion. "He'll take care of you. May Gayla and I count on the two of you to join us for dinner?"

Josh consulted Megan by raising a questioning eyebrow. She nodded imperceptibly. "Yes, thank you. We'll look forward to it," he said for both of them.

Terry was summoned to the check-in desk, which

was swarming with arriving guests and hustling employees. He waved them off, entrusting them to Greg's good care. Greg drove them through the paved paths of the complex toward the bungalow where they had been assigned rooms. Once away from the busy main building, Megan could only appreciate the serenity of the resort. As they cruised along tree-shrouded paths, the placidity was broken only by Greg's lively chatter.

"The swimming pools are through there. One is heated, the other isn't. That building houses the health club. There are exercise rooms for both men and women, showers, steam rooms, saunas, you name it. To get to the tennis courts, take the sidewalks marked with signs showing little tennis rackets."

"I don't know if I'll ever find my way around, but I'll have fun trying," Megan said. She was becoming uncomfortably aware that they were getting farther and farther from the central group of buildings. "How many rooms make up a bungalow?" she asked casually, hoping that her weak voice didn't give her uneasiness away. She could feel Josh's eyes roving over her face.

"Four," Greg said.

"Four," she repeated as though mulling over a vital piece of information.

"Yeah, but only the two you're in will be occupied this weekend."

Megan's mouth went dry. She dared not look at Josh.

Greg pulled to a stop outside the bungalow, which Megan decided was misnamed. "Cottage" couldn't begin to describe the enchanting quadraplex of apartments.

"Mrs. Lambert," Greg said, opening one door with a key and a flourish before standing aside. She went into the suite, which was decorated in blue, beige, and peach. From the bathroom, with its sunken tub, to the bedroom, with the king-sized bed and floor-to-ceiling windows overlooking the Atlantic, no detail had been overlooked. As soon as Greg had pointed out some of the more unique amenities and deposited her two bags in the dressing room, he left to show Josh to his adjacent apartment.

Left alone, Megan walked to the wide windows and opened the sheer curtains. A broad expanse of lawn extended from a private terrace outfitted with comfortable patio furniture. The grass was strewn with pine needles, which had fallen from the trees that separated her "yard" from the white beach.

It was a place made for lovers, a setting to appeal to all the senses, and she knew that if she weren't careful she would be doomed by this scheme of her own making.

As though her mind had conjured up his image, Josh was suddenly standing on her terrace, having walked around the wall separating it from his. Without thinking, she unlocked the sliding glass door, and he stepped inside.

"Forgive me for using the back door," he said. He didn't smile. His eyes were busy cataloging each feature of her face.

"That's all right. How's your room?" she asked on a thread of breath.

"Empty."

They came together in a sudden rush of movement. His mouth clamped over hers, while his hands scaled her back. A rowdy tongue destroyed her logic as it investigated her mouth with undeterred purpose.

"For once we're alone in a private place. There's no one to interfere. I don't want anything between us," he breathed against her neck as he divested her of the white jacket.

With no resistance from her, he walked them toward the bed. When they fell upon the quilted spread, her arms were looped around his neck, her hands in his hair as grasping and eager as his. He covered her only partially, giving himself space to explore.

With more discipline than she could credit herself with at the moment, he pulled the silk shell from the waistband of her slacks. The skin of his palm sliding over her ribs set every nerve in her body into bedlam. When his hand closed over her breast, she arched her back and cried his name softly against his lips.

"I've never forgotten how you feel." He took pleasure in her full breasts, which swelled over the lacy cup of her bra. His hand rotated over her slowly until her budding desire was cupped in the center of his palm. "Megan," he said hoarsely, "unbutton my shirt. Touch me before I die."

Her willing, anxious, eager fingers complied. She combed through the fine hair spread over the hard muscles and ribs. His breath stilled, then was expelled on an anguished moan. "Yes, yes," he growled before welding his lips to hers again.

The front clasp of her bra fell away. Like a blind man, he educated his fingers to the feel of her. The softly rising mounds, smooth flesh, and delicate peaks were stroked, petted, smoothed, teased by his curious fingers, which demanded to know all of her. He enticed her nipples to heightened passion with his skillful thumb.

"Josh, Josh," she whispered.

His other hand fumbled with the button and zipper of her slacks. As if ready to do his bidding, they came undone. The swathe of lace in the shape of panties provided little barrier to his sweet exploration. And then he was there, touching her, exciting her, arousing her with an undaunted intimacy that she knew should be forbidden, but which she couldn't deny him or herself.

It wasn't until he began to grapple with the zipper of his trousers and she felt the weight of his body lowering onto hers that she realized with stark clarity what would happen next.

She panicked.

It wasn't time. She hadn't set her ruse up properly. She had never meant it to go this far.

She began to struggle, and he ceased his movements immediately. "Megan?" he asked tenderly. "Megan, what is it? What's the matter?"

She groped for a plausible excuse why they couldn't make love right then. She said the first thing that popped into her mind. "James. I . . . we're betraying James."

Six

*T*here was only a heartbeat between the gentle kisses he had been planting on her forehead and the abrupt rising of his head. She had succeeded in jarring him out of his passionate daze. That it was taxing his willpower in the extreme was evidenced by his rapid, ragged breathing.

She knew he was looking at her, willing her to open her eyes, but she couldn't risk letting him see the truth—that she regretted calling a halt as much as he did. Instead she squeezed her eyes shut, until twin tears eked out from beneath her lids and rolled down her cheeks.

He raised himself off her and left the bed. The quiet rasp of his zipper being refastened in the silent room was as obnoxious as fingernails raking down a blackboard.

For a long while Megan lay perfectly still on her back, with her eyes closed. She wished he would just leave without saying anything. Her greatest desire was to curl into a ball, to bury herself, to wallow in regret.

She regretted ever having met him, danced with him, kissed him the night before she got married.

She regretted ever having consented to come here. If she'd been more adamant, Doug wouldn't have forced her to come. He knew how stubborn she could be. She could have worn him down by insisting she simply had too much work to do.

And she regretted . . . No! She wouldn't regret not making love to Josh. It was too dangerous to speculate on what it would have been like. The mere thought of it made her shiver.

"Megan, are you all right?"

"Yes, I'm all right." She rolled her head to the side and opened her eyes. He was sitting in a chair near the bed, looking earnestly at her. She knew she was a mess, that her eyes were red and her cheeks streaked from tears.

It was strange about those tears. Where had they come from? Their source frightened her, but she couldn't think about that now. If she examined it too closely, she might crawl onto Josh's lap and beg him to continue what they had begun. No, don't think about the loss you feel, Megan, she cautioned herself. "I'm sorry," she said aloud.

His knees were spread wide, where he sat leaning forward in the chair. Elbows on knees, his chin was propped on his fists as he studied her. "So am I."

She sat up slowly, closing the placket on her slacks

as unobtrusively as possible. "I . . . I didn't know I'd feel that way until . . ."

When her voice faded away, he said understandingly, "You don't have to justify that feeling to me or to anyone. I know there hasn't been another man since James. I'm glad. From now on I'm going to be the only man in your life." His softly spoken words and the indulgence with which he was looking at her made her unaccountably angry.

"Well, I hate to disappoint you, Josh," she said caustically. "I'm old-fashioned and not at all sophisticated when it comes to sex. If you wanted a playmate for afternoon romps, you brought the wrong woman, though I'm sure I can be replaced quickly enough." She vaulted off the bed and stalked over to the dresser, opened her handbag, and took out a hairbrush. She managed to drag it through her hair several times before it was caught and wrenched from her hand.

He lay the hairbrush aside and placed his hands on her shoulders. "I like the fact that you're principled— I prefer that word to old-fashioned—when it comes to sex."

"Only because I'm a novelty, compared to what you're used to. I don't know how to play these bedroom games. As far as I know, James was faithful to me even when he traveled. I was faithful to him. I can't help but feel cheap and dirty and guilty about . . . about sleeping with someone else."

"After three years!" he yelled, finally giving vent to

his temper. "Megan, for goodness' sake, you're not cheating on James. You're still very much alive, and you need a man to complement the woman you are." His hands closed around her neck; his thumbs massaged her collarbone beneath the silk blouse. "You need me."

When he touched her, she couldn't think. She had no comeback to this ridiculous argument anyway. She had thought it up only a few moments ago. What affected her more than she wanted to acknowledge was his willingness to try to understand her hesitation. Why wasn't he reacting violently to their thwarted lovemaking, tearing at her clothes in a lust-driven rage, making vile threats to get rough if she didn't come around?

His compassion would squelch her primary goal if she didn't fight it. Throwing off his hands, she cried out, "I loved my husband!" At least the desperation in her voice was genuine.

"I've no doubt you did," he said with a trace of annoyance. "Anyone who knew James liked him. He was a likable, lovable guy."

"You make him sound like a teddy bear or a puppy," she said indignantly. "You don't hold a patent on sex appeal, you know. James was a man, and I loved him as such."

The ticking muscle in his jaw testified to his suppressed anger. His lips barely moved when he asked, "Did you?"

"Yes."

"But if we had had more time—if we had met a month before instead of the night before your wedding—he might never have been your husband."

"Oh!" She clenched her fists at her sides. "You conceited, arrogant ass! One stolen kiss in the moonlight and you think I was ready to sacrifice everything for you. Well, I didn't, did I?"

"You were too stubborn then, just as you are now, to admit that you were making a mistake by marrying James after we had met."

Her chest hurt with pent-up emotion. His words came too close to the truth, and she dug in all the deeper to defend herself. "I'd had too much champagne."

He laughed harshly. "So now you've going to place the blame on being drunk." His voice dropped to a deceptively soft tone. "You kissed me, Megan, and that kiss forever changed how you felt about James, or yourself for that matter. Deny it all you want—to yourself, to me, to the world. You'd like to believe that that kiss didn't mean anything to you, but it damn well did. You know it, and so do I."

She was too enraged to speak. She stood facing him, her spine and arms rigid, her chin tilted up in defiance.

"Now, despite the rough spots that we have yet to iron out between us, I think you can see the advantages of keeping our problems to ourselves. So get your cute little rear end in that sinfully opulent bathtub and relax with a warm bath or take a cold shower and cool off your abominable temper. I'll pick you up in an hour and a half for our dinner with the Bishops, and you'd better be sparkling with good humor."

Megan was still seething with impotent fury when he left through the terrace door.

"You fool!" she cursed herself as she heeded his unasked-for advice and stood under the pulsing cold spray of the shower. She'd had the perfect opportunity to play the frightened, insecure female and she'd blown it. She could have had him in the palm of her hand, mistakenly thinking she was his.

If only she'd played up the part about feeling guilty, needing coddling and reassurance, he would have been as malleable as putty. Instead, stubborn and volatile as she was, she had succeeded only in raising his ire.

"I've got to pay more attention to the role I'm playing," she reminded herself as she applied her evening makeup. "Abominable temper," she spat, flinging an eyebrow pencil onto the marble dressing table. And how had he known that the bathtub in her suite was sinfully opulent?

As she dressed she reiterated her reasons for despising him, so that they would be clear in her mind. "Submission, Megan, submission. Be feminine. Flirtatious. Unopinionated," she muttered as she buckled the narrow strap of her sandal around her ankle.

She surveyed herself critically in the mirror. "Not

bad," she commented. Turning sideways, she sighed dispiritedly. "A little more bosom wouldn't hurt."

She'd chosen her dress because of its sensuous fabric and unusual design. It was a subdued white crepe de chine. The dress had a draped bodice front and back, which was barely tacked together at the shoulders, leaving most of her shoulders and all of her arms bare. The front dipped low but only hinted at what lay beneath the silky cloth. The full skirt swirled around her knees.

She pulled her hair back into a bun low on the nape of her neck and all but covered it with a silk camelia with green satin leaves. Diamond studs adorned her ears.

Ready well before the appointed time, she gathered her crocheted shawl and beaded evening bag and paced nervously, rehearsing what she would say and do and wondering if, when the time came, she'd have the nerve to say and do them.

Josh knocked on the front door.

Licking her lips anxiously, she crossed the room, her knees rubbery. She kept her eyes lowered for several seconds after drawing the door toward her. Then slowly, hoping she looked provocative, she lifted her lashes and looked up at him penitently.

"You had every right to stand me up."

She could tell by the quirking of his eloquent eyebrow that her contrition had taken him by surprise. Apparently he had thought she would still be hostile and explosive. That he looked devastatingly handsome in his dark summer-weight suit and pristine white shirt almost dissipated her anger totally.

She wet her lips again, this time deliberately. "Josh, I'm sorry about this afternoon. I—I wasn't ready for something like that to happen so soon." That, at least, was the truth. "I didn't know how to act, what to do."

He drew her close and pressed her head onto his chest. "Forgive me for coming on like an adolescent maniac. I bungled it, not you."

"No. I behaved stupidly, immaturely. I thought I was ready for . . . it. I guess I'm not. Not yet."

"I shouldn't have rushed you. You've barely had time to readjust your thinking about me, about us. Forgive my impatience. It's just that I've waited so long for you."

As he spoke, his mouth wandered along her hair-line. Now he tilted her face up to his. He kissed her softly, barely applying pressure to her lips, but being thoroughly intimate with his tongue, which entered the sweet hollow of her mouth. A laser of desire beamed through her body, touching each vital organ, the tips of her breasts, the center of her womanhood.

A yearning so strong that she had no choice but to obey it seized her, and her arms came around his neck. She recalled how it felt to lie with him, his body hard and demanding, hers soft and yielding. Wantonly, she rubbed against the tightness in his loins.

"My God," he grated as at last he pulled away.

"You're not making this any easier on my self-control, Megan my love. Let's go."

The fresh evening air helped to lift the warm stain from Megan's cheeks. Her own loss of control during Josh's kiss had shocked and shamed her. She welcomed the balm of the sea breeze to clear her head and cool her fevered skin.

Their stroll through the twilight was leisurely and solitary. The pebbled walkways were lined with flowering plants. Crepe myrtle trees were just beginning to bud. The camelias were glorious.

"They look nice with your dress," Josh remarked, indicating one of the shrubs which was loaded with blooms. "Here, wait a minute. Is anyone looking?" he asked mischievously before pinching off one of the vibrantly pink flowers.

Laughter, unaffected and natural, bubbled out of her throat at his prank. "What are you doing, Josh Bennett? Trying to get us thrown off the premises?"

"We won't be," he said, winking. "I've got connections. Turn around."

"Why?"

"Just turn around."

She offered him her back and immediately felt his fingers adding the real blossom to the silk one with which she had decorated her hair. "It took me a half hour to perfect that coiffure. If you mess it up—"

"Be still," he commanded. He tugged, adjusted, patted, then said a satisfied, "There. That looks great."

His fingers trailed lightly to the nape of her neck. "And this looks scrumptious." He pressed a kiss onto the velvety skin.

The damp patch cooled quickly in the night air and contrasted wonderfully to another hot application of his mouth.

"Josh." Megan sighed in spite of herself. The gentle swaying of the pine trees surrounding them was somehow sexually symbolic. The air, laden with flowery perfume, and the shadowy private path on which they stood, were a seductive setting. "Josh," she repeated, hardly aware that she spoke his name aloud.

"Hmmm?" His lips nibbled, his tongue licked, his teeth raked lightly along her fragile skin. He tasted her like the most lascivious of gourmets indulging lewdly in a sumptuous meal. "Let's forget dinner," he breathed from behind her. "Nothing could taste as good as you." His tongue made tiny, quick strikes on her earlobe.

His hips settled more firmly against her back. She lifted her arms behind her head to caress his hard cheek and masculine jaw. Her fingers teased the dark hair that curled over the tops of his ears and clung to her fingers as if with a life of its own.

"Sweet . . . Get closer to me," he murmured before lowering his hands to her sides. Suddenly he froze. "Good Lord," he gasped. His fingers had encountered, not the fabric of her dress, but the warm suppleness of her skin. Barely moving his fingertips, he confirmed that he was indeed touching the sides of her breasts.

He turned her slowly to face him, and bound her eyes with his. Without releasing her from that mesmerizing stare, he slipped the fingers of both hands just beneath the sides of her dress and caressed the plump outer curves of her breasts.

"I'm liking this dress more and more," he said thickly. Lifting one of her arms, he studied the structure of the dress, which had been designed with a man's appreciation in mind. The side was open to about two inches above the waist, leaving the tender underside of her arm and torso bare.

"I—I couldn't wear a bra with it," she said shakily. She had worn the dress deliberately to entice him, of course, but she had not planned her own reaction to his appreciation. She'd intended for Josh to learn at some point in the evening how her dress was fashioned, but she hadn't planned on its being this early, or on his taking such keen advantage.

"I can see that," he said on an unsteady breath. "Better than that, I can feel it." He brought her hand to his lips and kissed the palm. Murmuring against it, he said, "I love the dress, but, damn it, I'll be miserable all night. I'll want to kill any man I see glancing in your direction."

With a possessive arm around her shoulders and a proprietary air, he escorted her the rest of the way to the main compound. They were to meet the Bishops in the most elite of Seascape's four restaurants. Terry had wisely provided eateries to suit any taste or budget, from hamburgers to Continental cuisine.

The latter restaurant was located on the second floor and provided a breathtaking view of the Atlantic at dusk. Black lacquered tables were covered with starched white cloths. The chairs were upholstered in either royal blue or burgundy velour. Crystal shimmered in the candlelight; silver place settings sparkled; a sedate sextet played soft music from a small dais rising from a parqueted dance floor.

As they entered through etched glass doors, Terry rushed forward to greet them. "Megan, you look beautiful. Josh, how do you like it? Are your rooms sufficient? Are you having a good time?"

Megan and Josh glanced at each other and burst out laughing at Terry's nervous enthusiasm. "Yes, we love Seascape. Yes, the rooms are superlative," Josh assured him.

"And yes, we're having a good time," Megan contributed. "But we're hungry," she teased.

He smiled shyly. "I know I'm being ridiculous. Gayla told me as much. She says if I don't calm down she's going to lock me in our room. Come on, she's anxious to meet you."

Gayla Bishop was as contentedly calm as her husband was harried. Perhaps her serenity had been acquired after having borne four children, Megan speculated. She would never have survived otherwise, if all the stories with which she regaled Megan were true. The plumpish woman seemed not in the least affected by the size of her bank account and looked upon Seascape as only one of her husband's many outstanding achievements. That they adored each other was obvious as they all chatted amiably and sipped drinks.

When Josh had automatically ordered Megan white wine on the rocks, she had smiled at him privately. Without the least bit of self-consciousness, he covered her hand with his and gently stroked her fingers, even as he conversed with Terry about Seascape's three golf courses.

"I was even more anxious to meet you when I heard you were coming here with Josh," Gayla Bishop told Megan frankly. She leaned forward and whispered conspiratorially. "He's so damned good-looking. Of course I love my Terry to death, but I'm not blind or dead!" She laughed lightly.

"I'm here at your husband's invitation, not Josh's," Megan clarified. "Seascape commercials are running on the television station I work for. I'm overseeing the account."

"Oh, I understand, I understand," Gayla said with an impish grin that told Megan she didn't understand at all. Did everyone think she was only Josh's date for the weekend? For her plan to work, they must suspect much more.

"I really think it's time someone lassoed Josh

Bennett. It's time he settled down. Terry says I'm naive, but I'm so happily married I can't understand why anyone wouldn't want to be. I couldn't live alone, absolutely could not." She covered her mouth with a hand that was heavy with diamonds. "There I go shooting off my big mouth," she said abjectly. "I'm sorry, Megan. Terry told me your husband just dropped dead one day. You poor thing."

The loquacious woman's apology was so apparently heartfelt that Megan didn't take offense. "It's all right. Living alone's not so bad once you get used to it."

Gayla's brows arched expressively. "Well, if the way Josh looks at you is any sign, I'd say your days of living alone are numbered."

"But—"

"I've been telling that man for years, ever since he visited Terry and me on the boat one summer, that he'd better watch out. 'One day a woman is going to come along and knock you right out of your shoes.' That's what I told him. And, honey, you're the most likely candidate I've seen." Gayla paused to study Josh as he spoke quietly to her husband.

Megan had been rendered speechless. She didn't think it would do any good to try to set the record straight. She had the impression that once Gayla Bishop made up her mind about something, she didn't change it no matter what.

Gayla took a sip of her champagne cocktail and

continued. "I'll admit I've been worried about Josh. Ever since he broke it off with—"

"George, Ms. Wray," Terry said, interrupting Gayla's recital just when it had commanded Megan's full attention.

The developer stood up, as did Josh, to shake hands with a man Terry introduced to Megan as one of Seascape's investors, an industrialist from Savannah. They also greeted Laura Wray, who looked stunning in a floor-length sheath of ice-blue satin. It clung to her willowy figure and accented her fair coloring. She spoke to everyone in a refined, modulated voice and tilted her head up when Josh kissed her lightly on the cheek.

"Laura, as beautiful as ever," Megan heard him say.

"Thank you, Josh."

After they exchanged pleasantries, the couple moved away to join a larger group at another table. Terry and Josh excused themselves to circulate around the room, Terry asking Josh nervously to accompany him on greeting his guests. "I'm terrible at remembering names," he said, mopping his brow with a wrinkled handkerchief.

"Well, I almost got in trouble with my big trap again," Gayla said with a gushing sigh of relief. This time she gulped down her cocktail. "I was just about to speak that woman's name, and all of a sudden, there she was!"

Megan's hand shook slightly as she brought the

slender-stemmed wineglass to her lips. "Ms. Wray?" she asked on a high note.

Gayla was apparently too caught up in her own tale to notice Megan's agitation. "Yes. You knew, of course, that Josh was engaged to her."

Megan shook her head before she found enough voice to croak, "No." She cleared her throat and tried again. "No."

Gayla's cheerful, round face collapsed. "Damn! Terry's going to kill me. *Kill* me. He always cautions me about flapping my jaws. Well, shoot, you should know." She caught Megan's hand and squeezed it tightly. "They were engaged about three years ago. Then, out of the blue and for no reason I could ever see, he told us it was off. Just like that." She snapped beringed fingers.

"I don't recall seeing anything about it in the papers." The muscles of Megan's throat were playing tug-o'-war with each other, making it painful to speak and breathe.

"No. It was one of those brief affairs that died before it ever got started. Anyway, I was glad when Terry told me Josh had a new girl. A man like that shouldn't go to waste." She patted Megan's hand again before hailing her husband across the room. "Terry Bishop, come back and order me some dinner."

There were titters of laughter as Terry rushed back to his wife, apologizing profusely to her and Megan for keeping them waiting.

Josh slid his lean body into his chair and reached beneath the table to squeeze Megan's knee. "Miss me?" he asked, bending so close that his breath wafted over her lips.

Deeply distressed by what Gayla had blithely told her, she answered, honestly and almost inaudibly, "Yes." Could the tears welling in her eyes be detected in the candlelight?

Josh's index finger traced the delicate sculpture of her jaw. Eyes with more facets than cut topaz blazed into hers, then dropped to her chest as though he would burn through the cloth that dared to shield her breasts from his avid gaze.

She felt herself gravitating toward him and was saved from embarrassment only by Gayla's imperious, "What should we eat?"

Josh had the pressed duck, Megan the chicken with lemon sauce. Both voiced accolades to the chef, who had been lured away from a prohibitively expensive hotel in Nice, France. "Want to sample a bite of mine?" Josh asked Megan. He lifted a forkful of the succulent meat toward her mouth.

"I was hoping you'd ask."

He guided the fork to her lips, and she closed them around the tines of the fork. Slowly, her eyes glued to Josh's, she moved her head back until the fork came away clean. His eyes stayed riveted on her mouth as she chewed languidly. She didn't realize until she saw the dangerous glint in his eyes how clearly sexual her behavior had been.

Her tongue darted out nervously, fleetingly, to lick the corners of her lips. Josh's breath hissed through his teeth as his eyes came flying back to hers. She read the passion lurking in their golden depths, and her heart beat a triumphant tattoo. Or was it pounding out of fear?

The meal was pleasant. She enjoyed the Bishops' company. The only thing that marred the perfection of the evening was the wistful glances she saw Laura Wray sending Josh. He seemed to be oblivious of her, never, to Megan's knowledge, glancing at her. Yet each time Megan looked at the woman across the room, she was staring at Josh.

"Would you like to dance, Megan?" Terry asked as they were sipping liqueurs and coffee.

"Yes, thank you," she said enthusiastically. The melodic strains of the small orchestra had been haunting her throughout dinner, and more than once she had found herself swaying to the slow rhythm. She loved to dance and didn't have much opportunity to do so.

Josh returned the favor by asking a flustered Gayla to join him on the dance floor. As soon as another song started, Megan was claimed by a television executive from Charleston whom she had met at a sales conference the year before.

She was laughing at his story about one of their colleagues, when she glimpsed Josh dancing with Laura

Wray. The laughter was trapped in her throat as though a cork had been pushed into it. A knife of jealousy ripped through her. The fierceness of her jealousy frightened her. She'd never known an emotion to poison her this way.

The woman's head was tilted back, her blond hair sweeping the tapering hand that was pressed against her back. They talked, smiled, and laughed lightly. When the song ended on a poignant refrain, Megan saw Josh lean down and kiss Laura softly on the mouth. To hide her feelings, Megan chatted volubly with her partner as he escorted her back to her table, hoping what she said made sense.

Before she had a chance to sit down, she was pulled into a pair of arms, the strength and possessiveness of which couldn't be mistaken. Hate for the woman he'd just danced with so consumed her that Megan held herself rigid against him.

Soon, however, the spiciness of his cologne, the strength of the muscles that rippled against her body, and the lulling notes of the music all soothed her. She was caught up again in Josh's web of sensuality, and for the moment she didn't want to escape.

Driven by an irrational need to prove to him that she was as much a woman as the one he'd once asked to marry him, she adjusted the curves of her body to harmonize with his.

"I thought dinner would never end." His lips moved on her temple. "I couldn't wait to get my hands on you." Smiling with secret pleasure, she began to lift her arms around his neck. "Please, Megan, put your arms down. I don't want to fight off a gang of would-be attackers." He flattened her hand on his lapel, folding her arm between them and holding her other hand in his. She knew it was no accident that it lay against her breast.

Magically they moved with the music. The room, bathed in candlelight from brass sconces mounted on the walls and hurricane lamps on the tables, was filled with romantic ambiance.

Lazily, Josh's thumb honored Megan's full breast. The caress brought a tickling sensation feathering up from the pit of her stomach to the back of her throat and down again, deeper this time, to the very heart of what made her a woman. Her cheek rested against his hard chest, where she could hear the thudding of his heart.

She should be angry with him for not telling her about Laura Wray. She should scorn him for the indifferent way he cast women aside once he was through with them. But her arsenal of vituperations had been sealed up when he took her in his arms and held her to him as though she belonged there.

"It feels so good to hold you this way," he whispered, letting his mouth linger at the top of her ear. "To do this." The caress of his thumb on her breast was subtle, invisible to anyone else, yet from the currents it sent sizzling through her body, he could have been touching her in the most intimate way possible.

"It's driving me to distraction to think that one mere scrap of cloth is all that's keeping your breasts from my eyes." His other hand slipped to her waist and drew her closer still. "From my hands." He kissed her just below the ear. "From my mouth."

She trembled and pressed her face against his shirt-front. "Josh, you shouldn't say things like that to me here."

"You're right," he said, suddenly disengaging her. He braced her when she reeled slightly from the loss of support. "Since I intend to say a lot of things like that to you, I guess we'd better get out of here."

Seven

She was virtually dragged off the dance floor. They said a hurried good night and thank you to the bewildered Bishops and hastily left the restaurant.

"Let's walk on the beach."

Josh took her hand, and they strolled around the Olympic-sized swimming pool, where a few of the guests were still cavorting. To those they recognized, they called out rushed greetings. Others were up to their necks in the churning bubbles of the outdoor hot tub. Neither appealed to Megan at the moment. She sought only to be alone with Josh.

Nearly all the paths of the compound led eventually to the beach. Josh took the nearest one, which sliced across the broad stretch of manicured lawn, through the tall grass left growing on the gently swelling dunes, and down to the expanse of white shore.

"Oh, how lovely," Megan said reverently. They'd left the lights far behind and found the deserted beach in its natural state. With the surging tide, the moonlight kissing each foaming wave, and the wind carrying the ocean's roar, the scene seemed primitive, elemental, and unchanging.

"You're lovely," Josh cupped her head with one hand while the other closed around her throat. His mouth fused with hers, his tongue pushing through her yielding lips to nestle in the pliant moistness of her mouth.

The wind ripped strands of hair out of her neat chignon and whipped her dress wildly, but Megan was hardly aware of it. The heat of Josh's mouth, the hard strength of his body, were all the protection she required.

When he finally released her and stepped back, he glanced down at her high heels, which had sunk into the sand. "You won't get very far like that," he said, laughing. "Put your foot up here." He patted his thigh.

Caught up in his lighthearted mood, she wiggled her high heel out of the sand and lifted her foot to his thigh just above his bent knee. His strong, slender fingers closed firmly around her ankle, and he unbuckled the strap. The breeze billowed her skirt, providing him with an enticing view of smooth, trim thigh. It was funny how the elements were working with her to aid in Josh's downfall. The wind was tearing through his hair, and the irregular angle of that one eyebrow added to his devilish appeal.

Once she was rid of her shoes, they took a few steps along the beach. "I can't resist it," he said, sitting down on the sand, heedless of his expensive suit. He slipped out of his shoes and socks and rolled a double cuff on his pants legs. Standing up again, he shrugged out of his coat and unknotted his tie.

"You don't intend to go any further, do you?" she asked, teasingly.

"Only if you will too," he said suggestively.

"No way. I'd freeze."

His eyes slid down her body and, if she hadn't already been chilled, his gaze would have made her shiver. The crepe de chine was plastered to her, and the cool wind had brought her nipples to hard distention. "You wouldn't hear me complaining," he said boldly. She gave him a discomfited look that made him laugh, and he wrapped his free arm around her. Her shoes dangled from his fingers. "I want to walk in the surf."

"But I can't," she said, stopping again.

"Why? Too cold?"

"No, I'm wearing panty hose."

"So?"

"*So?* So that would feel terrible, and besides, they'll get wet."

"Not if you take them off."

"Josh!" She glanced quickly around. The beach was still deserted except for them. "I can't do that."

"Why?"

"Are we going through that routine again? I just can't, that's why. Someone might see me."

"There's no one to see you," he said, spreading his arms wide to make his point. "Except me. And I certainly wouldn't jeopardize my reputation as a gentleman and peep."

She eyed him warily. "You're not a gentleman."

"Oh? Well, then, I need to become one. Come on," he urged, "take them off." When she hesitated, he bent toward her and asked, "What's the matter? Don't you trust me?"

"Not a bit."

He only laughed, the wind carrying the sound away, but not before it sent chills of expectation down Megan's spine. Was anything about him not attractive? "Please," he said like a little boy asking for a second cookie, "I have my heart set on walking in the surf on this beautiful moonlit night. Please."

"Turn around," she said, resigned. When he complied, she reached rapidly under her skirt, hooked her thumbs under each side of the panty hose, and peeled them down her legs. "Okay," she said when she was free of them.

Before she knew what he was about, Josh had snatched the garment out of her unsuspecting hand. "Thanks for the souvenir," he said flippantly.

"Give those back," she demanded, hands on hips.

"Unh-unh," he retorted, stuffing the panty hose into his shirt.

"That's . . . that's perverted," she sputtered. Despite her feigned anger, the thought of so intimate a garment lying on his furred chest made her light-headed.

He wrapped his free arm around her waist and

pulled her against him once again. "I confess. Where you're concerned, I'm crazy. Now," he said with less patience, "can we walk in the surf?"

The water was cool, but not alarmingly cold, as it tumbled over their bare feet before returning to the sea. The capricious swirling of Megan's skirt against her bare legs intensified the sensations rioting through her body. Her blood seemed to pump with the impetuous tempo of the tide.

Josh matched his longer stride to her shorter one, and they walked in companionable silence until the lights of the compound became less distinct, looking like a cache of jewels that had been spilled onto black velvet.

"I didn't know you were once engaged to Laura Wray," Megan said at last, voicing the thought that had been uppermost in her mind all evening.

Josh's footsteps faltered only momentarily before he said, "Few people did. It didn't last very long."

"I saw you dancing tonight. You seemed very ... close." The words cost Megan a vast amount of pride, but some unknown impulse demanded that she ask about the extent of Josh's feelings for the newspaper editor.

"Laura's a lovely, intelligent woman. I like her. She's a good friend now."

Pangs of jealousy jousted in Megan's heart, and she tried desperately to quell them. *She* didn't want him. This moon-charted, star-studded stroll along the beach was only part of her plan. Events were falling nicely into place. People were seeing them together. An Atlanta photographer had taken their picture with the Bishops at dinner. It would be in the morning paper. In a few days she'd have Josh Bennett exactly where she wanted him—thinking that she loved him, when she really didn't. She put down her insane rash of jealousy as a side effect of becoming involved in the role she was playing.

"You seemed captivated by each other," she remarked with affected indifference. "Are you sure the flames aren't still burning?"

Josh stopped and turned to face her. "Not even a flicker," he said quietly. "Megan?" When she lifted her face cautiously to his, he went on, "There's only one woman who captivates me." His lips came down on hers firmly and surely, eliciting aftershocks that left her weak and trembling.

"You're cold," he said, mistaking the shivering of her body. "We'd better start back."

They changed direction, not having as far to go since their bungalow was between them and the main cluster of buildings.

"I called the office this afternoon. The Dixieland people couldn't be happier," Josh told her.

"Good. I feel guilty. I haven't given my staff a thought today. I suppose I should call them in the morning."

"You're on vacation."

"So are you, but you checked in. Your business means everything to you, doesn't it?" She knew better than anyone the unreasonable demands he made on his employees, though now that wasn't her reason for asking. She wanted to know what motivated him.

"My business means a lot to me, yes. I started with nothing and have made something. It's all I have to show for my adult life."

He sounded almost regretful, but she shoved that thought aside as ludicrous. Everyone knew Joshua Bennett was a man of driving ambition, to the exclusion of everything else. "Where did you grow up?"

"West Virginia. My father worked in a coal mine and died when I was ten. Black lung, a man-made disease. I swore that even if I had to starve, I'd never go into a damn mine."

Megan heard the iron determination in his voice and could visualize him as a boy, wild, embittered, unruly, and hostile. Yes, that description fit the man he had grown up to be. It came as a mild surprise to her to realize she hadn't known anything about his upbringing, yet she had known instinctively it hadn't been a privileged one.

"You were an only child?"

"Yes, thank goodness. Mother had a hard enough time keeping me fed. She cooked and waited on tables at a diner. Most nights she brought home leftovers for my supper."

They had reached the lawn in front of the bungalow.

By tacit agreement, Josh dropped his coat and their shoes onto the grass. Leaning his back against the trunk of a pine tree, he pulled Megan into the circle of his arms. His chin rested on the top of her head as he continued.

"One day between school and my job at a gas station, I went to the diner. One of the mine boss's sons was giving my mother a hard time about there not being enough catsup on his cheeseburger. He was a real jerk, a bully who lorded it over everybody. He was older and bigger than I was, but I hauled his tail off that stool and pounded the hell out of him." He chuckled softly, causing Megan's breasts to vibrate against his chest. "Nothing will ever give me as much pleasure." Placing a finger beneath her chin, he tilted her head up. "Nothing except making love to you," he whispered, and kissed her deeply.

"Where is your mother now?" she asked in a breathless whisper when at last her mouth was freed. Marveling over the sensuous talent of his lips, she outlined them with her fingertip.

The lips beneath her gliding finger became thin and hard with bitterness. "She died two weeks before I graduated from high school." He laughed sadly. "It was her life's ambition, to see me graduate."

"What did you do then?" Suddenly Megan was starved for information about him. She knew nothing about his life before the night she met him. Even the years since then were a wasteland of information.

Every time James had begun to tell her something about the man who employed him, she had adroitly changed the subject. Now, inexplicably, she was eager to know everything.

"I moved around, working at odd jobs until I had saved enough money to enroll in one semester of college. I talked a minister into letting me live in the basement of the church in exchange for doing janitorial and yard work. If there's a shred of decency in me, it's because of him and his wife, who fed me one meal a day and loved me in spite of my meanness. Anyway"—he sighed—"I managed to get through school, obtain a loan, and start my company."

"You're glossing over the difficulties. It couldn't have been as easy as that," she said gently, combing back a shock of dark hair from his forehead.

"It wasn't. I worked like hell." His grin split the dark shadows of his face with a white slash.

"What made you interested in advertising? A creative mind? An artistic nature?"

"Hardly," he said with a short burst of laughter. "I just learned by accident that I was a born promoter. I came up with ideas that worked, to publicize upcoming events on campus, even at the church I lived in. I'd get an idea, and describe it to an artist, who would make the signs and posters. I'd come up with the theme but delegate the busy work to someone else." He dropped a kiss on her forehead. "That's what I'm still doing."

145

"And it's paid off. You're very rich."

"Wealthy? Yes, I suppose so. But money never mattered much to me. It wasn't the lack of funds that galled me. It was the indignity one has to suffer because of being poor. When I looked down into the mess I'd made of that bastard's face—the guy who was insulting my mother in the diner—I swore to him and to myself that I wasn't going to let anyone run roughshod over me and mine again."

"There's hardly any danger of that. You're too strong." She knew that from experience. "You're the embodiment of the American dream. You have everything you want."

He grasped her face between his hands and raised it to his. "No, Megan. The thing I wanted most I've had to do without and only because I had no choice."

His mouth came down on hers ravenously, twisting, bruising, until he seemed to realize that she was all too willing to accept his kiss. Her fingers tangled in his hair and drew his head down closer to hers. Their bodies came together with unleashed desire.

While their mouths sought to appease insatiable appetites, Josh's hand smoothed down the underside of her arm until he found the sides of her breasts.

She moaned his name with a beseeching sound and, having that endorsement, he waited no longer to slip his hand beneath the airy material. Closing his hand over her breast, he kneaded it gently. He weighed it in his palm, measured its fullness, tested its sensitivity by gradually working his way to the crest that strained toward his caressing fingers.

"Let me love you, Megan. I want to see what I'm touching. I want to hold it in my mouth."

"Oh, Josh," she groaned. Her hands groped for the buttons of his shirt and pulled them from the holes. She inhaled his intoxicating scent and granted the wish of her fingertips to touch him. His hair was springy, his skin warm, his muscles firm.

She craved him. As his hands grew bolder in their seeking caresses, her senses clamored for fulfillment of the raging desire he'd sparked to life four long years ago. His lips as they branded her neck with kisses, his hands that had aroused her nipples to aching need, the love words he poured in her ear—all threatened to defeat her purpose.

Knowing she had to retreat now or be lost forever, she backed gradually away from him. Her hands were still on his chest, but they were pushing against it.

"Josh, no more, please."

His head thumped against the bark of the tree, and his panting breaths vied with the wind's impetus as he seemed to slowly come back to earth. His arms fell listlessly to his sides. His eyes were shuttered by thickly fringed lashes.

Suddenly Megan felt an overwhelming need to comfort him. She struggled to conquer it. He was the enemy. She had set out to defeat him the only way she knew how, by using the only weapon she possessed.

Sad stories of his youth couldn't alter her determination or color her opinion. He was a responsible man. No longer the victim of unfortunate circumstances, he made his own choices. He used and abused people. He deserved a comeuppance, and she was determined to give him one.

Yet all that was hard to remember when he opened his eyes and grinned crookedly at her. "I made a promise to myself that I wouldn't try to persuade you, after what happened earlier today. Why I made such a stupid promise, I'll never know."

The smile she gave him in return was wooden, but he seemed not to notice as he said, "You ought to be in bed. I've got a big day planned for us tomorrow."

The big day he had planned started at 7:00 A.M., when he knocked loudly on the glass door of her terrace. "Wake up, sleepyhead. The day's getting away from us."

"You've gotta be kiddin'," she muttered, opening one eye to confirm what she thought—it was much too early to get up. After all, she was on vacation!

"Megan!" Josh roared from behind the sheer curtains that were the only drapes she had drawn over the wide window.

She slung off the light covers, disentangled her arms and legs, stretched, and went to the window. Pulling the curtains aside, she glowered at him. "You've got your nerve," she mouthed through the sliding glass door.

"So do you, coming to the door dressed like that," he said with a lazy insolence that matched his stance against the glass. His amber eyes roved over her body, pausing at places that responded as if called to attention. The batiste, thigh-length nightgown couldn't hide the pouting of her nipples, which, she realized, showed as twin dusky shadows beneath the apricot fabric. She was further appalled to see that the matching bikini panties, rather than hiding her most private parts, only lured his eyes to them. "May I come in?" he asked in a hoarse voice.

She could no more have refused him than she could have sprouted wings and taken flight. Her eyes remained locked with his as she fumbled with the latch and slid open the door. He stepped inside and, with the sea breeze circulating around them, making a sail of the curtains, they continued to stare greedily at each other.

He was dressed to jog in a tank top and shorts. What man but Josh Bennett could get by with wearing bright red? she wondered. Yet the color heightened the nut-brown hue of his skin, while the scooping neckline of the tank top revealed his thick, dark chest hair in a blatant display of raw masculinity.

Megan longed to touch the hard curves of his biceps, naked but for the thin straps of his top. His long thighs, bulging calves, and finely formed feet were bare except for well-worn white running shoes. He wasn't a once-a-month runner. She knew he took it seriously.

"Good morning, little girl. Wanna go out and play?" he asked. His eyes traveled over her tousled head, an affectionate smile on his lips.

"My mother told me not to play with older boys," she said, taking up the game. Saucily, she spun on her heels and tossed her head, her nose in the air.

"You should have minded your mother," he said, grabbing the back of her nightgown and yanking her to a halt. His hand closed around her upper arm, and she was hauled against his chest with an impact that left them both breathless. Or was it the closeness of their bodies, which were dressed too scantily for them not to notice the prominent differences that made their eyes go cloudy? "Playing with boys my age can be downright foolhardy," Josh whispered.

His mouth met hers with a savagery tempered by tenderness. Lips gazed each other, clung, meshed. His tongue breached her teeth and touched the tip of her tongue teasingly, then skirmished with it until he was declared the victor and granted all the privileges that went with the title. Skillfully, leisurely, and thoroughly he investigated his conquered territory.

He lifted his head reluctantly, stringing tiny, wet kisses like a soothing lotion along her swollen lips. His hands slid down her arms, and he rubbed his palms on the sides of her breasts.

"I intended to exercise this morning," he murmured.

"And you should." Her lips were lying against the strong column of his neck, delighting in the scent of his after-shave lotion and the taste of his skin.

His hands clasped behind her waist, and he leaned back to look down at her. "But if I don't get out of here, and if you don't wipe that sultry expression off your face and put on a few more clothes, by the time I get through with you I won't have the energy it takes to crawl, much less run a few miles." He kissed her on the tip of the nose and dropped his hands. "You're coming with me, aren't you?"

"For a few miles?"

He laughed. "One mile?"

"Half," she conceded.

"That won't get you into a marathon."

"Thank goodness. Wait here and I'll change."

She hurried into the dressing room and closed the louvered door behind her. "How did you sleep?" she called as she peeled off her nightgown and panties. It made her giddy to think that she was naked just a few feet away from him. What would he do if . . . ? What a stupid question. She knew exactly what he'd do.

"I had a rotten night. Only a pair of panty hose to keep me company." She heard the springs of the bed creak, and assumed he was sitting down on it.

"Oh? I thought the accommodations were most comfortable." She paused in pulling on a pair of shorts to listen for his response.

A series of luridly colorful oaths came from the other room; then he said grouchily, "My ailment had nothing to do with the accommodations."

Feeling safe behind the louvered doors, Megan smiled like a gamin. "Nothing serious, I hope."

"I know the perfect cure. Come out here and I'll show you what it is."

By now she had put on her exercise bra—she worked out at a downtown health club two evenings a week—and a sleeveless T-shirt to match her shorts. Around her forehead she had wound a cotton scarf to act as a hair- and sweatband. Bravely she accepted Josh's challenge and stepped into the bedroom.

His back was against the padded, fabric-covered headboard of the bed, and he was sprawled in the rumpled indentation where she had slept all night. His relaxed position belied the feral look in his eyes, which left no doubt of the healing cure he had in mind.

Megan assumed a lofty air and placed her hands on her hips, dropping onto the bed the tennis shoes and socks she'd carried from the dressing room. "Well?"

He came bounding off the bed, tackled her around the waist, flung her to the bed and pinned her there with a heavy thigh. Her screech pierced the air.

" 'Well?' Is that what you said? 'Well?' " He gnawed the area between her neck and shoulder with his mouth.

"Oh, Josh, please," she half-laughed, half-shrieked.

"That tickles!" She squirmed, thrashing her arms and legs as much as he would allow.

"Ahh, be careful with those knees. We don't want to damage anything we may need later, do we?" He braced himself over her with stiff arms, and she lay still, with nothing but her chest moving as she breathed in great gulps of air.

His expression turned serious. "You're so gorgeous," he said with stirring softness. "Gorgeous and intelligent and sweet and sexy as hell." Gradually he lowered himself over her, letting her absorb his weight. His kiss was gentle. His lips played upon hers until she moaned in supplication. His teeth nipped her lightly. Then his tongue buried itself in the wet vault of her mouth. When at last he raised his head, he asked, "Are you ready?"

"Ready to what?" she asked in a low rumble.

His crooked eyebrow lifted in humorous query. "Ready to run."

Hot color rushed to her face. "Oh, to run. Of course, yes, run. Yes, I'm ready." He laughed. "Except . . . except for my shoes." She still hadn't recovered from having his entire body pressing her deeper into the mattress, their bare thighs caressing each other's.

"Allow me." Still holding her down with one leg thrown over hers, he picked up her socks. She propped herself up on her elbows to watch. "I like this toenail polish," he commented before leaning down to kiss her toes lightly. Straightening as he pulled on her sock, he added, "Almost as much as I like the outline of your nipples against that tight T-shirt." She didn't have time to gasp her surprise before he leaned back and paid the same homage to her nipples that he had to her toes, and all the breath deserted her body.

She remained stuporous until both socks were on and her tennis shoes had been tied with deft fingers. "There," he said, standing and pulling her to her feet. He slapped her on the behind, giving her no choice but to snap out of her trance. "I'll give you a head start."

After they'd been running for a while, it was obvious to Megan that she was a better runner than Josh had expected. He grinned at her broadly as she kept pace with him as they sprinted along the dawn-washed beach. It was still early, and they had it to themselves. After about a mile and a half, Megan reached her limit and began to fall back.

"Go on. I'll wait for you here."

He waved and continued running down the seemingly endless beach, until he was only a dark speck against the white sand. Megan slowed to a walk and allowed her pulse rate to return to normal slowly. Then she did sit-ups and stretching exercises on the sand, checking periodically for signs of Josh's return.

After she had gone through her regimen, she sat down on the damp beach, pulled off her shoes, and stretched her legs out in front of her. She stared out at the ceaseless patterns of waves playing across the water. How far he must have run, she couldn't guess, but he'd been gone well over half an hour when she saw him coming back.

His breathing was labored as he came jogging toward her, kicking up sand and tearing off his shirt. He tossed it in her direction, but she dodged the sweaty garment. "Come on," he said breathlessly, still running in place, but sweeping down to catch her wrist and pull her to her feet.

"What are you doing?" She laughed as she stumbled after him. He was heading toward the surf. "No!" she cried, trying to tear her hand from his iron grip.

"Why not? Great way to cool off."

"I'm cool, I'm cool." She was laughing so hard she could barely walk. How he managed to retain his hold on her and hop, first on one foot, then on the other, to take off his shoes, she never knew. "Let me go," she squealed one last time before he pushed her into the water.

They played in the surf until, exhausted, they lay in the shallows and let the tide bathe away their healthy fatigue and perspiration.

"If we had an ocean in Atlanta, I'd run on the beach every morning," Josh said, lying on his back and closing his eyes against the new sun. Megan longed to touch his chiseled cheekbones and the dark lashes that lay against them. The wet running shorts molded his form, detailing it for her curious eyes. The breadth of his chest, the flat plane of his stomach, the ampleness of his sex were all unselfconsciously displayed for her appraisal.

She rolled onto her stomach and rested her chin on her folded arms. "You're quite an exercise nut, aren't you?"

"Yep."

"Since when?"

"A long time. One of the first things I did when the company was large enough to warrant it and we were making enough money to afford it was to arrange memberships for all my employees in one of the downtown gymnasiums. I encourage them to go several times a week for an hour, even if they have to take off work early to do it."

Megan's head snapped up sharply at his words. She stared at Josh with incredulity. His eyes were still closed.

"James . . ." She licked her lips. "James never mentioned a health club."

Josh squinted against the bright sunlight. "I know. I urged him to go, Megan. He, more than anyone, needed the exercise. Every time I mentioned it, he put me off with a joke and a promise that he'd make the time. To my knowledge he never did."

Megan gazed at the long beach without seeing it. "Not to my knowledge either," she said quietly. She lay her head on her arms, letting the salt water wash over her body with a massaging motion

"Hey, are you asleep, or have you drowned?" Josh asked her long minutes later.

By an act of will she dispelled her solemnity. Rolling over onto her side, she smiled up at him. "Neither."

"Come on, then. I found something last night when I was walking off my . . . ahem . . . frustration. I think you'll like it."

They gathered up their shoes, her socks, and his tank top and struck off in the direction of the woods that joined the beach about a hundred yards from the shoreline.

"Where in the world are you taking me?" Megan asked as they tramped through the soft, springy undergrowth. With the monstrous trees towering over it, this foliage couldn't get much sunlight, yet it was brilliantly green.

"Right here," he said proudly, with a broad gesture. He bent at the waist in a courtly bow. Behind him stood a giant oak tree, its spreading branches draped with curly moss. Secured to one of the enormous limbs was a swing. The rope that held it was as big around as Megan's wrist. The wooden seat was about two feet long and a foot wide. The rope had been threaded through holes at either end of the seat and knotted underneath.

"A swing!" she cried in delight, rushing over to it. As she grabbed the ropes, she threw her head back to look up through the leafy branches of the tree. Sunlight dappled dark green leaves, which formed an intriguing pattern against the blue sky. "I love it."

Josh grinned smugly. He dropped his shoes onto the cushiony undergrowth and sauntered toward her. Pushing her away, he sat down on the wooden seat.

"I thought this was supposed to be my surprise," she said petulantly.

"It is. You sit on my lap." He patted his bare thighs.

"I can't swing like that. I'll fall off."

"No, you won't."

Grudgingly she moved forward and, turning her back to him, plopped down on his lap. For a moment he didn't say anything. When he did, it was with the utmost derision.

"Megan?"

"Yes?"

"You're right. You'd fall off that way. Turn around."

She sprang off him and whirled around. "You mean f-facing you?"

He pointed an index finger at her and closed one eye. "Now you get the picture."

Her eyes wouldn't obey her command that she not look down at his lap. Unerringly her gaze went to it. She swallowed a knot of apprehension. Just as she'd thought, his damp shorts clung tightly, making his sex blatantly apparent.

"Megan." He said her name softly yet so compellingly that she raised her eyes to his. She felt herself shrinking, becoming the size of her reflection in his eyes. The gold irises enfolded her, surrounded her, and she was inside him. Moving like one entranced, she stepped forward. With his guidance she placed first one leg, then the other, over his, until she sat on his thighs, facing him.

"Put your arms around my neck and hold on," he told her. As if in a dream, she obeyed. The muscles of his arms flexed as he took hold of the ropes. She felt the contraction of his muscles beneath her thighs as he took backward steps. He went as far back as he could go, until his body was straight and at a sharp angle. She held on to him tightly as his toes barely touched the ground.

"Ready?" he asked.

Exhilarated, she shouted, "Yes!"

He lifted his feet and they swooped through the air. Their laughter and cries of joy flushed a family of blue jays from its nest in the tree. One jay squawked angrily at them, but the wild beating of their hearts drowned him out.

When they swung outward, Josh's chest came forward to give them propulsion on the way down. Each time it came in contact with Megan's, she thrilled at the touch. Her damp T-shirt was stretched taut, providing him with a dazzling display of her breasts. The peaked tips were prominent evidence of her excitement.

On the backward arc, he leaned back and she hovered over him for timeless moments. During those suspended seconds, gravity pushed her forward until his masculinity was snugly tucked between her thighs.

The seesawing motion of their bodies sent all her senses into one melting cauldron of desire. The boiling emotions scattered her reason. She caught a handful of Josh's hair with one hand. Her ankles crossed behind his hips. Their eyes transmitted messages of passion until unbearable heat consumed them both.

When Josh let them begin to coast down, his mouth fastened onto hers. His arms were still holding the ropes, but even without their urging, she scooted higher up his body and pressed her breasts to his bare chest. They glided to earth slowly, but Megan's soul was still soaring.

At last the swing came to a complete standstill. Only then did Josh let go of the ropes and wrap his arms around her, one around her shoulders and the other around her hips.

His eyes remained closed as he rested his forehead against hers and breathed deeply. "My Megan," he whispered. Her lips drifted over his hard cheek, tangy with salt from the ocean. He spoke so quietly that she had to strain to hear him. "The night you married James, I thought I'd go mad."

Eight

*M*egan's heart seemed about to leap from her chest with its pounding. Wordlessly, motionlessly, they clung to each other. She didn't credit her ears with what she'd heard him say, but she couldn't help the riot of emotions that they incited.

At long last he raised his head and looked at her bleakly. "I got stinking drunk and stayed that way for about three days, living on drafts of whiskey taken at regular intervals."

"You were at the wedding." She didn't recognize the frail voice as her own.

"Yes. Sitting there listening to you promise to become another man's wife, to be for him all that that word entails." Balancing them on the narrow wooden swing seat, he lifted one hand to her face. With an exquisitely light touch, his index finger charted her face. "I don't know how I kept still and let it happen. Lord knows I wanted to run to the front of that church, steal you away from him, and take you for myself."

She rested her cheek against his palm and closed her eyes. "You knew I was getting married when we met.

You knew that when you followed me out to the summerhouse."

"Yes, and maybe at that point I was still only obeying an instinct. The minute I saw you, I felt like I'd been poleaxed right between the eyes, but I couldn't believe it. You . . . how old were you then? Twenty-five?" At her nod, he went on. "I was a good ten years older. I'd fought my way out of poverty. I was tough, mean, jaded. Falling for a slip of a girl at first sight didn't happen to brutes like me." His lips brushed hers lightly. "But once I kissed you, I knew that what had happened was real."

"I should never have let that kiss happen. I belonged to James."

"I knew that, but I didn't want to accept it. For months I refused to." He caught a strand of her hair and wound it around his finger. "Then I cursed myself for being a damned fool and started dating and bedding every woman I could."

He toyed with her T-shirt, seemingly fascinated when each time he pulled the damp cloth away from her breasts and let it go, it molded around them again. "You were like an illness inside me that wouldn't respond to treatment. No matter what I did, who I did it with, I ached from wanting you, Megan." His thick lashes lifted, and his eyes bore into hers. "I exercised immeasurable restraint in letting you go once. I'm not going to inflict that self-denial on myself again."

She was powerless to resist as he splayed his hands

hard and wide on her back and pulled her even closer. Like a branding iron, his mouth seared hers, burning straight through to her soul. He released her mouth only to trace a scorching trail down her throat with his lips. She let go of his neck and took hold of the ropes. Letting her head fall back wantonly, she leaned backward in open invitation.

His hands coasted knowledgeably over her breasts, and he fondled them with slow, sure motions that ignited a hundred fires in her body. His tongue flicked along her collarbone, then lower. It laved the curving swell over her breasts.

"Josh," she cried when he gently squeezed a rising nipple between his fingers before covering it with his mouth. Reflexively she arched against him, and knew instantly that he was just as aroused as she was.

"Ahhh," he groaned. He lay his head in the crook of her shoulder and released deep, shuddering breaths. Physical agony distorted the features of his face as he strove to regain control of his body. At last he sighed and raised his head.

"We've got to get out of here, unless you want to find yourself rolling in the clover," he said gently.

At that moment she had no qualms about making a bed of the lush undergrowth or a canopy of the oak. It was just as well Josh wasn't as impulsive. He stood up and let her slide slowly down his body until her bare feet met the ground.

"Besides," he said, bending down to retrieve their shoes, "I have a golf date with Terry."

An hour later he was standing over the space she had claimed on the beach as her territory. She lay face down on a large towel, which was scattered with the latest best-seller, sunglasses, a bottle of suntan lotion with maximum sunscreen, a small towel, a cooler containing three cans of soft drink, and a transistor radio—in short, everything she needed to spend the day on the beach.

They had returned to their respective rooms, showered, and eaten a breakfast of whole-wheat toast, poached eggs, and fresh fruit with yogurt dressing that Josh had asked to be delivered to his terrace.

Now he asked, "You're sure you don't mind if I leave you to play golf with Terry?"

She minded greatly that he was leaving her alone for the next several hours, but she looked up at him and smiled. "Go putt your little ball around the golf course. This is what I planned to do today anyway."

He looked terrific, in white slacks, a navy blue knit shirt, and golf cleats. What rankled was that she knew he looked even better without them in only a thin pair of running shorts. Her blood ran hot through her veins at the thought—and not because of the sun beating down on her back.

Her bikini provided little protection from the sun's burning rays. She had chosen it, hoping to begin a good overall tan. It was made of crocheted cotton yarn. The cinnamon color was almost the same shade as her hair, but without the copper highlights. Only the strategic parts of the bikini were lined with flesh-colored material. Narrow strips on the sides of her hips held the front and back triangles of the bottom piece together. A braided drawstring tied the miniscule cups of the bra between her breasts. Another tied behind her neck.

It would serve Josh right if she turned over and let him see the front, she thought wickedly. He might not be so eager to run off and play golf then.

Instead she shielded her eyes from the glaring sun and asked, "Will you do me a favor before you go?"

"Name it."

"Without getting sand in your shoes, can you rub some of this sunscreen on my back? If I don't protect against a burn, I won't be able to move for the rest of the weekend."

Dropping down beside her, he leaned over and growled into her ear. "That's no favor. That's a privilege. One I think most men would kill for."

His hands smoothed the rich emulsion on her back with strong, massaging strokes. Working his way down from her shoulders, he went beyond the thin string to the small of her back. Under his magic fingers, she relaxed until a heavy languor anchored her to the blanket. The lethargy was banished the instant his fingers slipped beneath the bikini panty.

"Josh!"

"Hmm?"

"You're . . . you're putting sunscreen in a place that will see no sun."

"Oh," he said, his fingers gently kneading her firm flesh. "Well, you can't be too careful."

That was something she would do well to remember, she reminded herself.

"Legs?" he asked softly.

"Uh, yes, I guess you'd better."

Squeezing the tube, he drew long white worms of suntan lotion down the back of her legs. Both hands closed around her calves to rub in the lotion. A warm, secure sensation wrapped around her heart. But when he knelt between her ankles and leaned forward to rub the cream into her thighs, the erratic drumbeat of her heart began again. Its pounding echoed off the hard-packed sand beneath her, making her acknowledge and absorb her own agitation.

His fingers climbed upward, his thumbs pressing into the soft skin between her thighs. Like heat-seeking devices, they moved ever closer to the very center of her which throbbed achingly. Her skin emanated heat. Her nipples knotted with tingling desire. When he slowly withdrew his hand, she was left with an excruciating longing that begged to be assuaged.

"All done." The unsteadiness of his voice matched her own uneven breathing.

"Thank you," she whispered.

"Are you sure you'll be all right? We're a distance

from the main building. Why don't you go to the pool? There'll be people around there."

"I'm a big girl," she said, propping herself up on her elbows before she realized how the position emphasized her breasts in the small bikini top.

"I can see that," Josh murmured, his eyes feasting on the provocative display. He cleared his throat and looked abruptly away. "I'll be back as soon as I can. Save me a place on the blanket. And for my peace of mind, if you should go to the pool, please change swimsuits first."

"Tell Terry hello for me, and have a good time." She smiled brilliantly, but she was swamped with disappointment as she watched him stalk across the sand and over the lawn toward their quadraplex to pick up his golf bag.

Dismayed by her momentary sense of loneliness, she stared blindly out to sea. Then the sapping heat of the sun, the sound of the surf, and the gently caressing breeze lulled her to sleep.

"Am I disturbing you?"

Megan pried her eyelids apart and allowed a slice of bright sunlight to penetrate. "What?" she asked, rolling over and sitting up, groggy and disoriented.

"Were you asleep? I'm sorry," the voice said.

As her eyes became accustomed to the glare of sunlight, the blurred image of Laura Wray came into focus. "Oh, hi, Laura," Megan said self-consciously.

She adjusted the straps of her bikini to provide herself with the maximum coverage. "I guess I dozed off, but I'm glad you awakened me." She glanced at her shoulders and saw the unmistakable pink that could herald a sunburn. "If I'm exposed too long, I burn."

"That's why I'm swathed in gauze like a mummy," Laura replied, smiling from behind fashionably large sunglasses and the hood of a turquoise, ankle-length, long-sleeved beach coat. "Do you mind if I sit down?"

"Of course not," Megan exclaimed, embarrassed by her lack of manners. She moved aside the articles littering the blanket, and Laura lowered herself gracefully down on it. "Would you like something to drink?" Megan offered, pulling the styrofoam cooler toward her. Terry had been foresighted to provided each room with one. "A cola?"

"Yes. I walked quite a distance down here."

After handing Laura one of the canned drinks and opening one for herself, Megan gazed down the stretch of beach. No one else was in sight. "Did you come looking for me?"

Laura sipped the drink and shook her head. "No. I was merely strolling along the beach. When I saw you by yourself, I thought this was a good time for us to get to know each other better. I admire you for the position you hold. Ever since we arrived, I've heard people talking about the outstanding job you're doing at WONE."

"Thank you, but I feel humbled by your saying that.

I admire your writing immensely. It must be fabulous to travel all over the world and get paid for doing it."

Laura shrugged and took another drink. "Yes, it is," she said thoughtfully. "Especially if you don't have anything else to do—husband, children, that sort of thing. You're here with Josh." She glanced up at the bungalow tucked among the pines.

Taken out of context, the two thoughts could seem unrelated, but, knowing Laura's history with Josh, Megan knew they were not. Why did she suddenly feel like the fallen woman confronting the saint? She had an impulse to cover herself, as though her near nakedness were obscene.

"N-not really *with* him. I'm overseeing Seascape's television advertising. Josh is their advertising agent." Megan found Laura's steady stare disconcerting. For good measure she added, "I've known Josh for years."

"Yes, I know," Laura replied in a tone that indicated she didn't believe for one minute that their joint interest in Seascape and the length of their acquaintance were the only reasons behind their being together. "Your late husband worked for him. Josh often spoke of you when we—"

She broke off in mid-sentence, and Megan finished it for her. "When you were engaged to him?"

Laura became visibly upset. "How did you know about that? Did Josh tell you?"

Megan understood her alarm. Like any woman, she wouldn't want her past failures exposed to what she considered to be the competition. "No, no," Megan said quickly. "Gayla Bishop mentioned it. I didn't know about it until last night."

Laura looked relieved, but she laughed mirthlessly. "Few people did. We broke off before it was announced. Josh"—she paused to lick her lips, and Megan panicked, afraid that she was about to cry—"Josh had a change of heart."

"That was beastly of him," Megan said with more hostility than she had intended.

Laura's reaction surprised her. "Oh, no. No, it wasn't. I appreciated his honesty. If he hadn't been forthright with me, we would have married, become increasingly unhappy, and then divorced with far more folderol than a broken engagement caused."

"How can you defend him? What he did to you only points up what an arrogant, selfish man he is."

Laura Wray studied her for a long moment, and Megan realized she had been too disapproving. "Arrogant?" Laura said musingly. "Yes, I suppose he is. But he's also kind. It caused him considerable anguish to come to me and tell me he wanted to break his commitment. He took all the blame on himself."

She smiled sadly. "As a matter of fact, by the end of the scene I was comforting *him*. And selfish? Yes, he is, but not only for himself. He's selfish for everyone he cares about. He had it very tough as a kid. What he has now he got through hard work. He'll never forget what it was like to be without. Still, he's generous to a fault—with material things and with himself."

Megan couldn't believe they were talking about the same man. Josh had always gone after what he wanted and damned the people who got in his way. She couldn't remember when he'd ever been denied anything. Everything he'd ever wanted . . .

No. There was one thing he'd wanted and hadn't obtained—her.

But surely Laura Wray's estimation was colored by her feelings for him. "You're still in love with him, aren't you?" Megan hadn't intended to ask the question; it had just popped out. To Megan's relief, Laura didn't seem to take offense.

"Yes," she said quietly as she stared at the horizon.

Megan traced a pattern in the condensation on her cold drink can. "Maybe there's hope that the two of you will get back together." The thought brought a crushing pain to her chest that she didn't want to analyze. Visions of Josh holding, touching, kissing Laura Wray—or any woman—with the same passion as he did her filled her with hatred. *Why?*

Laura shook her head and turned back to Megan. Her smile was gentle, reconciled. "No. Never. I have to be content to be his good friend." She stood up and dusted sand off the blanket where she'd been sitting. "I knew all along that Josh was in love with someone else. A married woman. In the end he admitted it to me. I think he'll always be in love with her."

Megan's heart plummeted, and her tongue became glued to the roof of her mouth. When Laura asked, "Will you be at the cookout tonight?" she could only nod "I'll see you then." Laura started walking back in the direction of the central compound, a tall, graceful, lonely figure.

Megan sat motionless, staring at the rolling waves. They brought to shore so much promise, rushing forward so eagerly, the magnificent strength of the ocean behind them. But they touched land only briefly, sparkling with lacy foam for only an infinitesimal moment, then receding, leaving nothing but debris in their wake. Was that the pattern of all life forms, a ceaseless, futile struggle for meaning?

What was she doing here? Why was she bent on carrying out a childish scheme for revenge? When it came right down to it, what was she seeking to accomplish? Who would get hurt the most? She had the unpleasant intuition that it would be she.

She jumped, startled, when a low, rumbling voice asked directly in her ear. "Can anyone join this party?"

Flattening a hand against her chest to still her wildly beating heart, she whipped her head around and bumped noses with Josh. "Ouch," he said before kissing her loudly. Instead of golf clothes, he was wearing a pair of maroon swim trunks. "Whatcha doin'?"

"Enjoying the peace and quiet."

He dropped down beside her and hooked his arm

around her neck, tilting her head back with his other fist. "If that's a veiled hint that I should leave you alone, you're out of luck. I ran their tails all over that golf course to get back to you as quickly as possible." His lips formed an unbreakable adhesion with hers. He milked her mouth with gentle suction, as though to draw all her sweetness into himself.

"You didn't play well?" she asked with what little breath he left her.

"Hell, I won! I always play to win, or it's not worth the game."

His words alarmed her, terrified her, but she had no chance to evaluate them as he drew her into another soul-splintering kiss. Gradually he lowered them to the blanket, until they were reclining, their arms and legs entwined.

"How's your back?" he whispered against her breast.

"A little pink, but it doesn't sting." He certainly had no problem with sunburn. His body was toasted a dark bronze all over. His chest hair grew in a whorling pattern that intrigued her. She traced it tentatively with her fingers. The crinkly mat spread wide at the top of his chest and tapered down his torso to a darker, smoother line that disappeared into his trunks. His navel nested in that line, but when her exploring fingers reached it, she couldn't bring herself to touch him.

"It doesn't bite," he murmured. Taking her hand

under his, he guided it over the deep dimple on his abdomen. "You have an open invitation to touch me at any time, in any way, any place you want. I give you carte blanche of my body."

The words made her dizzy with erotic thoughts, and she buried her face in the hollow of his shoulder. Her curious fingers threaded through his dark satiny hair and investigated the small indentation until his breath caught.

"Lie down," he instructed.

She complied. Rampant desire had made her weak. Her eyes closed against it. She let her body relax. She preferred not to think of it as surrender.

Taking up the bottle of suntan lotion, Josh said, "I'd never forgive myself if I neglected to protect your front as well as your back." The deep, rolling sound of his voice beckoned her into a deeper lassitude.

His hands were those of a gifted sculptor as they glided over her stomach and abdomen, applying a generous amount of lotion. Fingers that were strong and evocative massaged along the line of her bikini panties. She was disappointed when he didn't take the expedition farther—until she felt the drawstring of her top give way to his quick tug.

Her eyes flew wide as he moved aside the wisp of fabric and bared her to the sky. He was leaning close, gazing down into her eyes, "Shhh," he said soothingly. Tenderly his mouth kissed hers before he rose. She closed her eyes again, in time to hear a blasphemous whisper that was somehow reverent.

"My God, Megan, you're beautiful. I've envisioned you a thousand times, but you . . . you're . . . exquisitely made."

She felt the two pools of lotion he squeezed on the tops of her breasts. Working first one side, then the other, he smoothed the emulsion over her chest with languid motions. Occasionally he whispered a compliment, but his hands said more than words. He worshiped her through touch. His fingers conveyed the message that she was a masterpiece worthy of his admiration.

When all of her had been covered, except what she yearned most for him to touch, he withdrew his hands. Her eyes pleaded with him when she opened them. She needn't have worried. He was pouring lotion into his palms and rubbing them together. When they were thoroughly creamed, he lay them on her breasts. She gave a long, low moan, and her knees came up involuntarily.

His hands rotated slowly over her breasts. Her nipples, rubbing against his palms, flowered with desire. He raked his lubricated thumbs over them. "Josh," she sobbed.

"So delicate. So pretty."

Gently he gathered her lush breasts in his palms and molded her upward into cones cupped in his hands. Her fists knotted at her sides and, senselessly, she rocked her head back and forth. Low noises vibrated in her throat, and she heard herself repeating his name in a loving litany.

When he lowered his head and took one dusky nipple in his mouth, her back arched off the blanket and her hands tore at his hair. "Yes, yes," she urged.

But he refused to hurry. His lips fanned back and forth across the distended peak until she thought her veins would burst. His tongue dipped repeatedly to bathe the tender, swollen crest with the nectar of his mouth, until it shone wetly.

Her hips writhed with the fundamental beat of a pagan rite. The tempo increased with each squeezing movement of Josh's mouth on her breast, with each flicking lash of his tongue. When she thought she could bear no more, he covered the center of throbbing desire between her legs with his palm, pressed deeply and rhythmically, and drew her nipple into the hot, liquid cavern of his mouth.

Her world exploded with a shower of light.

"Why did you do that?"

She lay curled against him, their damp bodies glistening. His hand combed lazily through her hair as her head was pillowed on his chest. "Because you've never been aware of, or at least sure of, yourself as a sexual creature. One's sexuality is nothing to be ashamed of, Megan. Misusing it, yes. But we were designed to seek and find sensual pleasure with each other."

She nuzzled her face against him shyly, and he chuckled softly. "One lesson at a time is enough," he said, retying her top. "Come on. I'd better get you inside before you're burned to a crisp."

He helped her gather her belongings; and they walked back to the bungalow arm in arm. At her terrace door he turned her toward him. "I'll give you an hour. Unless you'd like me to come in and wash your back when you shower."

She shook her head. After what she'd just experienced, she needed time to think, time to sort things out. What Laura Wray had told her about Josh's being in love with a married woman hadn't begun to make sense to her before he'd come back and tripled her confusion about her feelings for him. Everything was in a muddle.

Things were getting out of hand, and she didn't know how to regain control. She only knew that right now she couldn't stand naked beneath a shower's spray with Josh and not beg him to touch her and kiss her the way he had on the beach. Time, space, distance—all were essential for her at this point.

"I'll see you in an hour. I assume the cookout is casual."

He nodded, but she could tell his mind wasn't on either the upcoming party or what he would wear. He cupped her face between his palms. "I've tasted you now, Megan, and it only whetted my appetite. I want all of you."

Before she could utter a sound, he had gone into his own suite.

The cookout, held on one of the wide lawns, *was* casual, but in true Seascape fashion it was carried off with élan. Vast charcoal pits contained untold quantities of sizzling barbecued ribs and beef. Mounds of ice kept pink boiled shrimp ready to be peeled and dunked into spicy sauce. On long tables covered with red-and-white-checked tablecloths were platters of fried chicken, corn on the cob, steaming okra gumbo and seasoned rice, baked yams, juicy watermelon, relishes to appeal to every taste bud, biscuits, and corn bread. As if that weren't enough, hot peach cobbler and pecan pie were available to satisfy a sweet tooth.

After the meal, Josh suggested that they take a walk in Harbor Town. Megan agreed readily, and they set off in a car Josh borrowed from the resort.

Complete with its own lighthouse, Harbor Town was a commercially developed complex located on the harbor of Calibogue Sound. The man-made harbor had been designed as an imperfect circle, to preserve one of the island's massive oak trees. Acting as a sort of a mascot of the island, the tree was strung with tiny white lights. Entertainers performed nightly on a makeshift stage beneath its branches.

After window shopping along a row of exclusive boutiques, Josh and Megan paused to watch the show. A professional singer strummed his guitar in an attempt to keep time with two young boys he'd called up on stage. They were giggling and getting in about every third word of the ridiculous song, but the audience loved it. Adults and children alike shouted with laughter over the impromptu performance coaxed out of the two boys by the young singer.

"That one on the left is a real corker," Josh said. "You can tell by the devilish glint in his eyes." In unguarded moments like this one, he was a different man from the busy executive who was reputed to pull no punches in a business deal. His teeth shone in the dim light. His hair, stirred by the breeze when they had taken their walk along the marina, lay about his head in dark tousled strands that tempted Megan to touch them. The thought that came quietly to her rocked the very foundations of her soul, and she pushed it quickly aside.

"Takes one to know one," she said, gouging him in the ribs. "I'll bet you were a regular hellion when you were seven."

"When I had time to be," he said pensively. He speared her with a look from his amber eyes that meant he demanded the truth about what he was about to ask. "Why didn't you and James have a baby?"

Startled, she floundered. "Well . . . there . . . there

was hardly time. He . . . he died a little past our first anniversary."

"Had you planned to have children?"

Why she didn't tell him it was none of his damned business she didn't know. She heard herself answer, "Yes, sometime in the future we planned to have a family."

Josh's whole body seemed to sag with relief. Though he had draped an arm around her shoulders, she hadn't realized how tense he'd been until she felt the rigid muscles relax against her. "I wanted to have kids." He wasn't looking at her now, but at the two youngsters hamming it up on the stage.

Speaking around the hard lump in her throat, Megan asked, "Why didn't you marry and have them?"

"I was close once, but"—he shrugged laconically—"things didn't work out."

"With Laura." He nodded tersely. "She's a lovely woman, Josh. I like her."

"I didn't know you knew her." He turned away from the stage and faced her. She had his total attention again.

"I don't really. We visited today while you were playing golf. She talked about you."

"What did she say?" he asked quietly, though Megan could hear him even over thunderous applause as the boys returned to their beaming parents.

"That you were a kind man. That you regretted having to hurt her. That you were unselfish."

"Did she tell you why I had to hurt and disappoint her?" She nodded, but couldn't speak. "Why was that, Megan? What did Laura tell you?"

"She said you were in love with a married woman." The words scraped past her throat, pricking it like barbs.

"That's right."

Oh, Lord, why was he doing this to her? It didn't matter, it didn't matter. The statement reverberated in her head, but it had no meaning. It mattered more than she could have imagined. The revelation brought more pain than she'd ever known.

"I'm still in love with her."

"I see."

"No, you don't, but you're getting close." His enigmatic words brought her eyes up to his. His scarred brow was arched in what she could only interpret as mischievousness. There was a curl of suppressed laughter at the corner of his mouth. "She's no longer married."

Suddenly rage roiled through her, taking with it every misplaced tender emotion that had been collecting for the past two days. Her back stiffened. "Then why have you put the big make on me? Why didn't you bring *her* with you this weekend and leave me in peace? You're loathsome, do you know that? A mean, sick—"

He gripped her arms tight and shook her slightly to stop her tirade. "Megan, stop it!" he commanded. She turned her head away and squeezed her eyes shut.

His grip became tighter. "Didn't Laura tell you when I broke our engagement?"

Still refusing to look at him, she said acidly, "No. I didn't want to know. I didn't care. I *don't* care."

"The day after you buried James."

Nine

As she brought her head slowly around to face him, her mouth formed a moue of incredulity. She opened her eyes wide as she stared up into his smiling face.

"You mean . . . I . . . ?"

His eyes, sparkling like gems as his hands lightened the pressure on her upper arms, congratulated her on her brilliant deduction. "I meant what I said earlier today. I didn't take kindly to your marrying James. I had just found the woman I'd been looking for all my life. That you were about to become another man's wife didn't keep me from loving you, only having you." He steered her away from the crowd, which was breaking up now that the singer was doing his finale for the evening. "Let's go home," he suggested softly.

As they walked back to the car, he continued to explain. "About eight months after your wedding someone arranged a blind date for Laura and me. I wasn't enthusiastic about going. I wasn't enthusiastic about anything during that time." He hugged her tighter. "But I liked Laura's pleasant disposition and the fact that she didn't make any demands on me."

He unlocked the passenger door of the borrowed car, and Megan slid inside. In the brief seconds it took him to come around to his side, she drew in several deep breaths. *It couldn't be. It just couldn't be! Was Joshua Bennett actually telling her that he loved her?*

He started the ignition and navigated the car out of Harbor Town before he spoke again. "I began seeing more of Laura. I wanted children. I wasn't getting any younger. She expressed a similar desire to settle down and have a home and family. Your marriage seemed to be solid. I thought you were lost to me forever. I asked Laura to marry me."

The night was absolutely black, unrelieved by any sizeable moon. The stars winked brightly overhead, but they could hardly penetrate the network of tree branches in the thick woods lining the two-lane road.

Megan was grateful for the darkness. It hid her features from the man who was killing her with every word. It was a painless death, a marvelous one, yet she was dying just the same.

"Some intuition, I don't know what, made me ask Laura to keep our betrothal quiet for a while. Then in a few weeks, before we even made our engagement public, James was dead."

"And I was free," Megan whispered.

He parked the car as near the bungalow as possible. The cessation of the motor's throb sent a blanketing silence over them. "And you were free. The day after the funeral I told Laura I couldn't marry her. I thought she was entitled to an explanation. I didn't identify you, but I guess she figured it out."

He turned toward Megan, his clothes rustling against the car seat. His fingers sifted through the windblown hair lying against her cheek. "I knew it would take a long time, Megan, for you to accept me as anything but an interloper, a womanizer, an opportunist."

He shook his head in wry amusement. "That kiss we shared in the gazebo was one of the high points of my life, yet I cursed myself daily for it. You pegged me as a man who would dally with his friend's fiancée; you couldn't see me in any other light. You let your low opinion of me be known all too well each time I tried to contact you after the funeral. I finally realized that the harder I tried to see you, the more stubborn you were going to be."

He kissed her swiftly on the brow. "That's not an indictment, only a statement of fact. So, as hard as it was, I backed off and waited. I granted you three years. I was willing to wait."

Conflicting emotions battled inside Megan. She didn't know whether to rail against him, tell him he was accurate about her unaltered opinion of him, or succumb to the persuasive touch of his fingers trailing the lacy border of her sundress, which plunged seductively between her breasts. His lips at the corner of her mouth were relentless in their persuasion.

She never made a conscious decision. When he turned her toward him, she melted against his heated length. As much as the confinement of the car would allow, she molded her body along his, feeling his passion against her thigh and knowing that hers was just as strong.

"Don't make me wait any longer, Megan," he urged in a horse whisper.

He helped her out of the car and hurried her across the stretch of lawn. His arm was around her waist, cupping her breast lightly where it lay bare beneath the navy-and-white dotted swiss. They stumbled across the yard, laughing nervously at their eagerness.

They pulled up short when they saw two shadows sitting on lawn chairs at the front of the quadraplex. One of the shadows stood up, and Terry Bishop's voice called out to them. "There you are. Gayla and I were just about to give up on you. We thought a game of bridge would be fun."

The Bishops thought it would be fun until three-thirty in the morning, when a gloating Gayla gathered up the penny winnings for her and her partner, Megan. Looking at each other wistfully, she and Josh said a chaste good night.

They got a late start the next morning, sleeping in after their long evening. Since it was their last full day on Hilton Head, they wanted to cram in as many activities as possible but not wear themselves out before the grand formal banquet that night.

Josh called room service and had breakfast catered to Megan's patio. They wanted to take advantage of the amenities of Seascape, yet remain as private as possible. "What should we do first?" he asked, his teeth sinking into a crisp, cool slice of honeydew melon.

"I haven't tried out that mammoth pool," she said. His shirt was open, and the morning breeze stirred the hair on his chest. She envisioned her own breath blowing on it softly to see what tantalizing displacements she could make. It was an enchanting daydream.

"The pool it is, but I hope the suit you wore yesterday isn't the only one you brought."

"No, why?"

Without releasing her eyes from his, he rose from his chair and came around to her side of the small glass-topped table. Without the least compunction, he placed his hands over her breasts, which were unfettered under the loose caftan of rainbow-striped muslin. He leaned over her until his mouth was at the back of her ear. "It's all right for you to entice my baser instincts, but I don't want you enticing anyone else's. I don't intend to share these with anyone."

Hours later, blushingly reflecting on his words, she wondered why she hadn't taken exception to his propriety air, as she once would have done. Formerly her back would have bowed and her hackles would have risen and in dressing him down her tongue would have been as quick and as deadly as a viper's. Instead she had basked in the heat of his possessive claim.

After lounging at the pool and soaking up a couple hours' of sun, they toured the tennis courts. But rather than opting for a match, they checked out a bicycle built for two and struck out along one of the myriad bike trails that crisscrossed Hilton Head.

After several hilarious minutes while they tried to match each other's timing on the pedals, they got the hang of it. Beneath the trees, the bike path was shady and the breeze cool.

"You're not nearly as uncoordinated as I thought you were at first," Josh told Megan over his shoulder. He had taken the front seat, bragging that he knew better how to steer.

"Watch out for that dip!" she shouted. He whipped his head around in time to avoid catastrophe, but their recklessness set off another round of playfully insulting banter. At a secluded spot on the trail, Josh braked the bicycle and hauled her off. He propped the bike against a tree. "Let's take a walk."

"Isn't that what one gangster says to another gangster when he parks the car beside the woods?" she teased. Despite her suspicions, she thrashed along behind him through the forest of trees and undergrowth.

"Yeah. Prepare yourself for the kiss of death."

He braced her against a tree and secured her there with his own body. One arm closed around her waist while the other hand supported her jaw. His mouth came down on her firmly, completely, hotly.

His tongue probed her mouth with delicious thrusts, alternately forceful and gentle. When hers joined the play, boldly investigating the inside of his lips, his groan of satisfaction was like a sweet symphony in her ears. Her fingers traveled up and down the muscles of his back and, after several expeditions, her hands rested at his waist.

He had placed their feet so that one of his knees was snuggled between her thighs and one of hers between his. They both were wearing shorts, and static crackled along Megan's nerves, shocking her, electrifying her. Josh moved his knee slightly, and the soft hair sprinkling it tickled her sensitized skin. When she slid her thigh upward, he moaned her name and buried his face in the curve between her neck and shoulder.

"Megan, that feels so good. Do it again. Higher." When she obliged him, his mouth opened ardently over her throat and his tongue stroked a message of love. "Your skin is so soft against mine," he rasped. "I can't wait to have all of you naked beneath me."

He pulled back to look at her, and his eyes went straight to her chest. She had pulled on a pair of shorts over her maillot, and the peacock-blue nylon did not conceal the shape of her breasts and their impudent crowns. Josh ducked his head and kissed one button-like nipple. His lips turned inward, and he plucked at it gently.

"Oh, Josh, please." She didn't know if she was begging him to stop now or never. Perhaps her action spoke more eloquently. Her hands slid down to grip hard the flexing muscles of his buttocks as his hips rotated over her. He pumped against her rhythmically. She found a bare patch of skin on the back of his thigh and squeezed tightly.

"Sweet heaven!" he cried, and backed away from her. For long moments he gulped in air and blinked his eyes as though to rid them of an obscuring veil.

When his reason returned, he grinned down at her with chagrin. "I'm going to grow very old and very gray very fast if we have too many more of these close calls." He heaved a sigh. "*But* I don't want to make love to you for the first time on a bed of pine needles. We'd better go back to the bike." As he took her hand, he mumbled, "It's a long walk back to Seascape. I hope nobody's stolen it."

Indeed, when they came through the last barrier of trees, a couple was scrutinizing the bicycle. There was no chance of their stealing it, for they were each on one of their own. They were surveying the edge of the woods with concern. When the young man saw Josh and Megan emerging, he said in a friendly fashion, "We found your bike deserted. Everything all right? No one hurt or anything?"

"Naw," Josh said expansively. "She only had to tinkle and was too scared to go in the woods by herself."

Megan squealed a protest and kicked him soundly in the shin. The other couple pedaled away, laughing as Josh danced on one foot, holding the other leg, and Megan rattled off all the reasons she thought him diabolical.

As Megan walked into Seascape's Grand Ballroom, she saw that the chandeliers were subtly lit, so that they barely shimmered above the dozens of tables covered with powder-blue linen cloths. Each table was graced by a centerpiece of spring flowers in varying colors.

No longer covered with suntan lotion, but with expensive imported fragrances, the guests at Seascape's grand opening had discarded their play clothes and swimsuits and donned their finery.

Laura Wray, in vermilion chiffon, looked like an angel only slightly fallen from grace. At Terry's insistence, Jo Hampson had been flown in for this night. She wore a copy of a Valentino blouse that was made solely of white organza ruffles, and a red taffeta tulip skirt. It wasn't an outfit Megan would have chosen for the woman's overripe figure, but Jo couldn't look dowdy if she tried. They greeted each other warmly, and Jo haphazardly filled Megan in on what had happened in the office during her absence. Gayla Bishop trailed yards of beaded gold satin that didn't need the strands of diamonds hung around her neck.

Megan felt like the most stunning woman in the room when she met Josh's ardent gaze. When he had escorted her in, a hush had fallen over the room. "Damn those wolves," he'd growled. "I wish their eyes would fall out of their heads. Don't you have a scarf or something?" But his querulousness hadn't bothered her.

As with all the new items she'd bought for her wardrobe before leaving on the trip, she'd purchased this dress because of its sexiness. The tight long sleeves and bodice were black crepe. Where it attached to the tulle, it was cut into petal shapes that seemed to have barely climbed up an invisible vine to cling to her breasts. Beneath the sheer tulle, her skin, sun-kissed now, shone warm, and inviting.

She wore black satin high-heeled sandals. Her only jewelry was the diamond studs in her ears. Her hair was pulled to the top of her head in a seemingly careless knot. Soft, curling tendrils lay coyly on her neck.

Her flustered hand now reached up to tuck a vagrant strand of hair back into her topknot in a gesture meant to cover her nervousness. She had wanted everyone to notice her and Josh together, but now that the time was here, she wished they weren't so public a couple.

Apparently Josh did too. Once they had circulated and said their hellos, he chose a table away from the others, near the back of the room, where the lighting was dimmer.

"Dance?" he asked softly, and pulled her slowly into his arms. Once they were absorbed into the mass of other swaying couples, he said into her ear, "I really didn't want to dance, because then I can't look at you. But it was the only way I could think of holding you and getting away with it."

She was caught up in the magic of the beautiful room, of the music played by a string orchestra, of the night that was softly tropical. Most of all, she was enthralled by Josh.

He was a paragon of masculinity, in his black tuxedo and pleated shirt with onyx studs. He'd been dressed like this the first time she'd seen him, and the sight of him affected her just as strongly now as then. Now she knew that the passionate nature only hinted at beneath the austere clothing was real.

Now she knew the texture of his hair, which was silvered at the temples but carelessly, boyishly styled. She knew the cut of the tuxedo wasn't deceptive, that the broad muscles it intimated were actually here. She knew well the feel of his hard chest as it conformed to her soft shape.

"Move . . . ah, there that's it. Yes, right there."

Megan caught her breath sharply. With the merest pressure of his hand on her back he had positioned her to cushion the iron proof of his need.

"Now close your eyes and imagine that we're not

here at all, but lying naked on your bed. I'm loving you in time to the music. You're just about to take me inside you. And we move, slowly at first, then faster. We make love, again and again."

Megan's cheeks flamed and her heart pounded at his audacious words. By the end of the dance she was drunk, inebriated by his masculine essence, intoxicated by the picture he'd painted. He led her back through the maze of tables, his dark scowl discouraging any other man who might consider himself a potential dance partner for her.

Like an industrious spider he continued to spin his web around her throughout the interminable dinner. Because six other people were seated at their table, they had to carry on a conversation, but the others were unaware of the silent communication being exchanged by covert looks and secret touches.

Megan might have planned for tonight to be the culmination of her scheme. Obviously Josh had. He rarely took his eyes off her, and his golden eyes sent a message to her heart that it couldn't fail to decipher.

Finally the house lights were dimmed and everyone's attention was drawn toward the head table, where Terry Bishop began to speak. Josh took advantage of the distraction to lean over and kiss Megan on the mouth. Her lips opened under his as the petals on her dress opened to hold her breasts. Without so much as disturbing the color that tinted her lips, his tongue slipped between them to rub against the tip of hers.

When he pulled away, his voice was rough with emotion. "I love you, Megan. Marry me."

For a moment both of them were too spellbound to realize that they were once again the center of attention. Terry Bishop had blared Josh's name through the microphone on the podium. "Don't be shy now, Josh," he said. "Come on up here and let me and the stockholders present you with a token of our appreciation for the fine job you've done in promoting Seascape."

Everyone was applauding. For the first time in her life, Megan saw Josh ruffled. He looked at her bleakly, shrugged helplessly, straightened his bow tie self-consciously, and stood up. She watched him, still stunned motionless by his unexpected proposal, as he made his way to the head table.

His hand was shaken heartily by Terry and all the stockholders. Gayla kissed him soundly. Photographers snapped his picture. He was presented with a set of gold-and-diamond cuff links. He handled it all with humility and aplomb, then stepped behind the microphone and began to speak in a deep, stirring voice.

All of a sudden Megan had to get away. Without stopping to consider, she slipped out the back door of the ballroom and ran through the compound as fast as her high heels would let her. The truth had dawned on her—no, had struck her like lightning—and she had to be alone.

Indeed, lightning was striking all around her as she

ran down the pathways toward the bungalow. The wind destroyed her hairdo, but she was heedless of it. Tears flooded her cheeks as she continued to run. There was a burning pain in her side from running and a pain in her soul from what she knew now to be the irrevocable truth.

She reached the quadraplex in record time and fumbled in her beaded bag for the key. Once inside, she all but ripped the black dress from her body, as though it were a cloying shroud, and peeled the panty hose down her legs. Naked, she went to the dressing table to pull out what pins were left in her hair. Punishingly, she raked a brush through it.

The need to escape pressed upon her, bringing with it irrationality and panic. She must escape from herself and from the man who would come looking for her when he discovered she was gone. He mustn't find her tonight. He mustn't. She was too weak, too susceptible. If he found her . . .

Where could she hide? As if in answer a bolt of lightning zigzagged from the low clouds seemingly into the heart of the turbulent sea. Josh wouldn't look for her on the beach, not in this storm. Only a fool would go near the water during an electrical storm. But then, she was a fool.

She pulled on her bikini trunks but, thinking she might be too cold with the ocean wind howling, she substituted a soft, baggy sweat shirt for the bra. Within seconds she was out the terrace door and racing down the slope toward the beach. She ran from even a hint of light. The frequent blue-white flashes of the storm were her only illumination.

Far from her bungalow she sat down in the damp sand, pulled her knees up, and lay her forehead against them. Bitter tears scalded her eyes and wet her cheeks.

I love him.

The truth filled her mind despite her efforts to deny it. She had loved him long and well. She had loved him from the first moment she'd seen him, over four years ago. She had loved him far too well to marry another man, far too well to be considered a truly faithful wife, far too well to carry out a stupid plot for revenge. Whom was she avenging? James? Herself? Everything that had once been so clear to her was now a tangle of mixed emotions, a jumble of truths, half-truths, and misinterpretations.

Engulfed by remorse, she crumpled onto her side in a heap and sobbed bitterly. It wasn't Josh who had been brought to heel, but herself. The role she'd played for the past few days was the role she'd always wanted to play with this man but had never allowed herself to assume. The startling truth was that everything she'd done, she'd done because she'd wanted to, not because she wanted to bring him down. All the while convincing herself that she was lying to him with her seductive allures and affectionate banter, she had instead been lying to herself.

"You're a fool, Megan Lambert," she cried aloud.

"Didn't it ever occur to you that you'd fall into your own trap?"

For an indeterminate length of time she lay there on the beach and wept. The wind whistled ominously around her. Lightning popped and cracked, eerily lighting up the entire horizon or ripping through the curtain of clouds to momentarily weld together sea and sky. It might have started raining or it might have been salt water spraying on her cold skin. She didn't know or care. To the elements she was impervious. She knew only of the gnawing agony deep inside her and the emptiness that lurked on the outskirts of her soul, threatening to suck her into its fathomless void.

"Megan!" Her name sounded torn from an anguished throat. She heard it only a moment before she felt the vibration of running footsteps in the wet, hard-packed sand. Then strong hands were gently turning her over. "Megan?"

She opened her eyes, and the pain-riddled eyes that gazed down at her, searching her face, squeezed tightly shut in relief. His hair was whipping around his head in the wild wind. His tuxedo coat and tie were gone. So were his shoes and the studs that buttoned his shirt. The wind tore at the fine white cloth, pulling it away from his body, whose strength championed the storm's fury.

Kneeling in the sand, he grabbed her to him, wrapping his arms around her and all but cutting off her breath. "Don't ever do that to me again. I thought. . . . I thought. . . . Lord . . ." He rocked her back and forth in his arms, warming her. His lips covered her face with frantic kisses while his hands traversed her body anxiously.

"What made you do it, Megan? Why? Why did you run away from me? From *me*?"

His haggard expression revealed his agony and opened up the floodgates of her love for him. "I—" No, she couldn't tell him about her stupid plan for vengeance. He thought her signs of growing love had been natural, not engineered. They *had* been, so there wasn't any reason for him ever to know of her plot.

"Hold me, Josh, just hold me. I love you," she cried, throwing her arms around his neck.

He lifted her and carried her up the gentle incline toward the bungalow. The wind and rain lashed out at them but only gave him reason to walk that much faster. He passed through the open glass door and rushed to ease her down on the bed.

"Are you all right?" he asked, lifting the wind-ravaged, rain-plastered hair away from her face.

"Yes, yes," she sobbed, grabbing his hand and bringing his palm to her mouth.

He left her only long enough to lunge to the terrace door and slide it shut. Belt and trousers and underwear were discarded as he returned to the bed. She had used that time to fling the covers back and lie down on the melon-colored linens.

His eyes blazed into hers as he shrugged off his shirt

and came naked to the side of the bed. His sex was bold in its declaration of need and desire. The wild disarray of his hair, the fierce expression in his eyes, the harsh breathing that came through his lips, gave him a primeval bearing that set her blood racing to every erogenous zone of her body. With the most primitive of instincts she longed to satisfy the lust of her mate.

Her hands went to the bottom of the sweat shirt. Her eyes locked with his as she slowly and alluringly eased it over her breasts. Pausing to gauge his reaction, she pulled it over her head and stretched, her body forming one sleek, taut line of sexuality. She tossed the garment to the floor. Then, lifting her hips an inch above the mattress, she wiggled out of her bikini trunks.

A muscle in his jaw twitched spasmodically, and his eyes darkened. With a hand that trembled visibly, he reached down to test the texture of the auburn tuft. She purred her desire.

In an instant he was stretched out on top of her, and they fell on each other as if they were dying of thirst. His fingers plowed through her hair, capped her head, and held it possessively while his mouth ravished hers. His tongue plunged into her mouth, driven by hunger and the desperation to claim ownership at last.

Her hands opened over his back, rubbing hard the muscles that bunched and relaxed each time he moved over her, driving their bodies to a greater level of passion.

"This isn't the way I planned it," he said, gasping.

"I was going to go slow ... savor ... oh, Lord ... touch me there again."

"Please, Josh, now," she pleaded as her hips arched up to meet his thrust.

He buried himself in the moist welcoming silk of her body, and their cries of ecstasy rivaled the roar of the wind outside.

"Say you always wanted this." His choppy words matched the rhythm of his body's movement.

"I did."

"Say you fell in love with me that first night."

"The moment I saw you."

"Ahhh. I love you, Megan."

"I love you, Josh."

The storm outside was nothing compared to the tempest that raged between them. It was wild and free and furious and quickly spent.

Deliciously languorous, they regained their breath. She smiled against his lips, and he opened his eyes, regarding her drowsily. "Something's funny?"

She shook her head slowly. "I don't remember ever being so exhilarated or so exhausted."

He levered himself on his elbows and looked down at her. "I was rough. Did I hurt you?" His eyes touched her with loving concern.

"No," she said, investigating the scar in his eyebrow with her fingertip. Her lips parted with surprise when, feeling him nestled deep inside her, she realized that his desire hadn't been fully quenched.

"I'm sorry," he said commiseratingly, and made to move away.

"No!" she said, with such emphasis that he laughed softly before kissing her.

This time their voracity had been appeased and tenderness reigned. His lips moved over hers soothingly. He dragged his tongue along her lower lip, flicking lightly at the corners of her mouth until she squirmed beneath him with mounting desire.

Hands and mouths moved restlessly, never getting enough, striving for closer contact, thrilling to each blissful discovery. She lost her equilibrium when he rolled them over so that she was lying on top of him.

"I'm awkward," she said apologetically. "It's been a long time." And never like this, she could have added.

"You're perfect. Move up."

She felt forlorn. "But—"

He smiled slyly and lifted her off him. "It'll keep," he promised with words and glowing eyes. "Come up here."

With his warm hands cupping her bottom and directing her, she inched up his torso, reveling in the feel of his hair-roughened skin. When she was braced above him, his hands adored her breasts, lifting them for the avid inspection of his eyes. He filled his hands with their full warmth and squeezed gently. He pressed them against the wall of her chest, then let them fall and smiled up at her with wicked glee. She could laugh with him, for it made her exultant to know she pleased him so.

He brushed his thumbs across the dusky crests that were swelling again with awakened need. While his thumbs performed the delicious aggravation, he studied her face. "When I do this, your eyes become the most mysterious shade of green and your lids lower. You don't really close your eyes; you only hide them. I find it incredibly sexy."

When his hands moved slightly, she begged him breathlessly, "Please don't stop."

"Not even to kiss them?"

She bent her head to sigh against his lips. "Kiss them if you must."

His mouth closed around one budding nipple and suckled sweetly. Even as his jaw flexed and relaxed, his tongue nudged and circled until she was delirious. He gave the same unselfish treatment to the other breast as she massaged his stomach with her undulating hips.

Securing her against him, he eased them to their sides. Taking her hand in his, he guided it down his body. He watched her reaction closely, but she felt no hesitancy or fear when her questing fingers found him.

"You've been a part of me for so long that I can't remember a time when you weren't." The golden eyes closed and his breath came out in a shuddering exhalation when her fingers grew more confident. "Megan, every breath I've taken . . . every heartbeat for the last four years . . . has belonged to you."

Shyly, lovingly she whispered, "You feel so good . . . here." His throat vibrated with an animal groan. "Here." The word barely left her lips as her fingers tenderly honored him.

"If you think it feels good to *you* . . ." With a stroking hand, he gently parted her thighs and curved his palm over the center of her pleasure. He moved it in circles of increasing pressure. Fingers delicately probing found her moist and inviting. The secrets of her body were revealed to his curiosity.

They brought each other to the peak of fulfillment time and time again, but held it back, prolonging the torment only to heighten the release. As his fingers worked their magic, he bathed her breasts with his tongue. When she did the same to him, his whole body went rigid.

"Megan?"

She lay her thigh over his, and as they looked deeply into each other's eyes, he pressed into her to the very gate of her womb. Her hips climbed slowly onto his as he rolled to his back. Though this was a first for her, she seemed trained in the art as she moved above him. He encouraged and praised her with his hands encircling her waist, his thumbs skating over the auburn down and fondling her breasts lovingly.

When the tumult came, they were smiling at each

other, celebrating each other, loving each other with spirit as much as with body.

"Josh?"

"Hmm?"

"Are you asleep?"

"Are you kidding? When you're doing what you're doing? Not a chance." His chuckle was a rumble in her ear, as it lay on his chest. Her idle finger was circling a puckering, hair-whorled nipple. Their legs were entwined, their bodies touching everywhere they possibly could. Her hair made a coppery cape over his throat.

She stopped her provocative caress and lay her fingers flat. "I'm serious." His hand stopped its gentle stroking of her derriere and slid upward to cover her back protectively.

"Tell me," he demanded softly.

Drawing a deep breath, she said shakily, "I'm sorry for being so unfair to you all these years. I was wrong about you. I blamed you for the night you kissed me."

"I *was* to blame. Who did I think I was, to kiss another man's bride? At least the way I kissed you. It wasn't the most noble thing I've ever done."

"But I let you kiss me. I *wanted* you to."

He smoothed her hair. "That's the only reason I let myself do it. I thought that you couldn't help what happened between us any more than I could."

"I haven't been able to admit it to myself until now.

I lashed out at you, harbored anger, made you out the villain because I wouldn't admit my own guilt."

"You were a faithful wife to James," he said quietly. "If I had thought there was the slightest chance you might not be, I'd have come after you. I'd have said to hell with conscience and moral conviction and friendship."

She shuddered and snuggled closer to him. "I wasn't always faithful in my heart. If you had made an overture, I'm . . . I'm not sure what I would have done."

"You'd have sent me packing, just like you did the night before your wedding. That's why I loved you, Megan. If you had kissed me without feeling guilty, I'd have probably forgotten you within weeks. You'd have been no different from so many other women I'd met.

"But you *were* different," he went on. "So wonderfully different, with your righteous indignation following the most sexually explicit kiss I'd ever experienced. The contrast bewildered and elated me. I knew you were the woman I wanted, the woman I'd always love, whether I could have you or not."

She raised herself up to kiss him softly on the lips. He caught a strand of her hair and looped it through his fingers, toying with it even as she lay her head down again on his chest.

"I blamed you for James's death," she confessed in a small voice.

"I know. That was the hardest thing to take, because

I had no recourse. Anything I did you would have interpreted as arrogant selfishness. I bided my time as long as I could."

"If anyone's to blame for James's death, it's me."

"Only James is to blame."

"I should have seen to it that he took better care of himself."

"He was an adult. *He* should have seen to it."

"If I'd loved him the way I should have, I'd have badgered him to slow down, to stop smoking for good, not to drink so much. I should have insisted."

"If he had loved you the way he should have, you wouldn't have needed to." Her head came up to look at him. "Didn't you ever think of that, Megan?" He framed her face with his hand. "He had a responsibility to you. He knew he was living too hard and too fast, because you, I, everyone told him he was. But he was too cocksure to believe it. He knew his blood pressure was dangerously high. I didn't send him out on martini lunches; he went. I didn't like his late evenings with clients because I knew that meant you were alone."

A lone tear trickled down her cheek. He captured it with his thumb and spread the dewiness across her lips. "You're no more to blame for James's death than I am. His own compulsive drive to succeed at the expense and exclusion of everything else, even his own health, is what brought on that coronary."

She sniffed back the remaining tears and smiled. "Thank you for that."

He smiled softly. "Don't mention it." His thumb skimmed along her bottom row of teeth.

"I transferred all my guilt to you," she admitted. "I saw only what I wanted to see, heard only what I wanted to hear. I saw only your vices and was blind to your virtues." She lay on her back, urging him to his side with a compelling hand on his shoulder. "I'm not sure you have any vices."

"Oh, I have plenty." His eyes began a lecherous trek down her body. "One being . . ."

"Yes?" she hummed when his hands joined in the carnal activities his eyes had initiated.

"One being a naked lady with cinnamon-colored hair, perfect breasts, satiny skin, pink nipples that . . ."

Megan knew that the night was far from over.

Ten

She woke to the sound of her shower running and tuneless whistling. A smile played about her lips, becoming full-blown. Suddenly she laughed out loud and hugged the pillow that retained the scent of Josh's cologne. She buried her nose in its soft depth and inhaled deeply.

Had she ever known contentment like this? Never. Had her body ever been so satisfied? Never. Had her mind ever been so expanded, her senses so alert? Never. Had she ever so looked forward to a new day? Never.

Having had very little sleep, she didn't know why she wasn't exhausted. Instead, tiny capsules of energy were exploding inside her, filling her body to overflowing with enthusiasm for living.

She swung her naked legs to the floor and bounded out of bed, intent on joining Josh in the shower. Indeed, he had his nerve, using her shower without first asking permission! She laughed again before assuming a perturbed expression and stalking toward the bathroom, where the whistling was increasing in volume.

She was brought up short by the strident ringing of the telephone. "Damn," she cursed before lifting the receiver to her ear and saying an impatient good morning.

"Uh, good morning, Ms. Lambert. This is Barnes."

Megan's brow wrinkled with puzzlement. Whatever could he want, calling long-distance at this time on a Sunday morning? "Hello, Barnes."

"I guess you wonder why. . . . You see, I was really calling Mr. Bennett, but there was no answer in his room. I knew I could count on your giving him a message."

Her heart slowed after having lurched in panic. Had Barnes known Josh was in her shower at this very minute? She wasn't ashamed of it; she just didn't want it to be made public yet. "What kind of message?" she asked.

"Well, it's kind of complicated," he began.

"Try it out on me." She shifted her weight impatiently from one foot to the other. Damn it, she didn't want to talk business; she wanted to jump in the shower with Josh, to caress with lathered hands the body she now knew so well.

"Well, one of Josh's men, his name is Clancey—his last name, not his first. Anyway this Clancey is in charge of the new Air South campaign. You know they're ready to launch a new fleet of airplanes to—"

"I know all about Air South's expansion and the ad campaign that will go with it. I also know that Josh's agency is handling their advertising. Now, what's the message for Josh?"

"This guy Clancey was at a party last night and got slightly sloshed. Actually, he got very sloshed. Anyway, seems Josh came down hard on him just before he left for Seascape. It's not the first time. I've heard Clancey bad-mouthing his, quote, 'high and mighty' boss before. No one pays any attention. I mean, everybody complains about their . . . uh . . . their . . ."

"I get the point, Barnes," Megan said dryly. "Please get to yours."

"Well, last night was different. He was really vindictive, you know? He threatened to take the ad campaign and sell it to Powell Associates, which is—"

"Josh's chief competitor," Megan finished in a hushed voice as she sank onto the bed. Her mind, catapulted out of her impatience with Barnes, was now churning with the possible repercussions such an embezzlement would have on Josh's agency. It happened, though rarely, when an ad man from one agency worked on a campaign and then auctioned it to the highest bidder. Such espionage could bring ruin to an ad agency.

"Are you sure about this, Barnes? You're not exaggerating, are you?"

"No. Clancey was drunk, but he knew exactly what

he was saying. His wife was there. She kept begging him to shut up before he ruined everything. No, he meant it."

"Why would you call and tell Josh about this?"

She could imagine the chagrined look on Barnes's face as he sighed. "I guess I feel I owe him. He didn't have to warn you about the Dixieland account. He could have let me hang myself, and it would have been no skin off his nose. As it was, well, he was responsible for my getting chewed out, but I needed chewing out."

Had it not been for her concern about Josh's business, she would have smiled. As it was, she said tersely, "Don't talk about this to anyone."

"I won't."

"I'll be back in the office tomorrow. We'll talk then." She'd almost hung up when she heard him again.

"Ms. Lambert?"

"Yes?"

"I had a date with that woman who was giving me a hard time."

"And?"

"She won't be doing that anymore."

"You set her straight?"

"No, I saw the light. I can do better."

Megan did smile then. "I always thought you could."

"Thanks for . . . well, you know, for everything."

"No. Thank *you*," she said, referring to his tip on the traitor, Clancey.

She was just replacing the receiver when two hard arms came from behind her to wrap around her waist and an avid mouth adhered itself to her neck. "That better have been a female caller, and do you know just how saucy your little rear end is?"

"Oh, Josh," she said, whirling around to face him. It suddenly occurred to her that she had the ammunition that she'd have given anything for even a few days ago. She had the power to totally defeat Josh if she wanted to. Withholding this information about Clancey's betrayal would cause a serious setback to his career. He'd face public ridicule for letting such a precious account slip through his fingers. He'd lose tens of thousands of dollars in revenue.

Right there on the tip of her tongue was the secret that, left untold, would assure her of a revenge greater than any she could have dreamed. By smiling beguilingly up at him and wrapping her arms around his neck, pressing her body to his, and passing off the telephone call as a wrong number, she could lead him like a lamb to slaughter—innocent, unaware, incognizant of the disaster that was waiting for him.

But Megan didn't even entertain the thought. She knew only an urgent need to help the man she loved.

"Something terrible has happened, Josh."

His mouth swooped down on hers for a hard kiss.

"You got pregnant last night? Don't worry. I'll marry you. I hope it's twins."

She tore her mouth free from his persistent lips. "Please. I mean it."

"Who was that?" he asked, snapping his head up, instantly alert to her distress. He gripped her arms.

"Barnes."

The irregular brow shot upward. "Barnes!" he said scoffingly, with no small amount of relief. "Don't tell me. His girl friend's left him again."

"Josh, listen." Her hands wrapped as far as they could around his biceps and shook him slightly. "You have a man named Clancey working for you."

"Yes," he answered with a puzzled frown.

"He's going to take all his work for the Air South Airline to Powell Associates."

He stared at her for a moment, his face expressionless. "What?" he asked at last, his voice a disbelieving whisper.

"He and Barnes were at the same party last night. Clancey got drunk and started spouting off unflattering comments about you. Barnes said he was disgruntled over some argument you'd had with him and was threatening to take his ideas to your competition."

She didn't know what to anticipate, but it wasn't the booming laughter that shook the ceiling. Josh collapsed on the bed, pulling her down with him. She was so dismayed by his absurd reaction to the disastrous news that she was almost unaware that he hadn't bothered to dress after his shower. His body hair was still slightly damp.

"I didn't think Barnes was that ingenious," he said, wiping tears of mirth from his eyes.

"Ingenious? Josh, don't you see—"

"Don't *you* see. This is Barnes's way of getting me back. He probably even had a spy here who tattled on us. He had the bad grace to call at this time of the morning, hoping to interrupt something." His arms closed around her back and drew her hard against him. "We won't let him, will we?"

But she pushed the heels of her hands against his chest, her arms stiff. "Barnes isn't like that. He wasn't lying."

"I'm not saying he was being malicious," Josh said in a conciliatory tone she found highly irritating. "I'm just saying he's playing a little joke on us, paying us both back for the hand-slapping we gave him."

She pushed off the bed, stomped over to a chair where she'd left her caftan, and pulled it over her head. "This is no joke," she said tightly.

"All right. So he heard someone griping about me and took his mutterings and ran with them, built a mountain out of a molehill."

"I think you should consider Clancey's threats as more than mutterings."

Josh propped up on his elbows, nonchalant in his nakedness. "Megan, why are you getting angry?"

Again his tone annoyed her. "Because you're

implying that my employee is either a spiteful sneak with a warped sense of humor or an imbecile. If you think I'd hire such a person, then I have a fair indication of the credibility you give me as a businesswoman."

"That's not true."

"The hell it isn't," she flared. "Have you or have you not argued with Clancey?"

"It wasn't an argument. I told him his copy for the print ads stank to high heaven and gave him two weeks to revise it."

"And you question his holding a grudge? I know how you can put people down. Apparently Clancey's had enough."

Angry in his own right now, Josh rolled off the bed, picked up his underwear from the floor where he'd shed it the night before, and tugged it up his legs. Megan's mouth grew dry as she watched him adjust himself to fit comfortably in it.

"Clancey knew that copy was pure crap and needed changing. Usually he's a good man, with creative ideas. But too often he starts thinking of himself as a prima donna, and he can't tell good from bad because his ego gets in the way. I've taken him to task before and he always comes around. He's loyal. He'd never go over to the competition."

She ground her teeth. "You're so arrogant, so damn sure of yourself. I'm amazed at your self-esteem. Is everyone in the world supposed to share it, to think you're somebody special?"

He cast a sly glance toward the bed. "You do."

The blood rushing to her head made her dizzy, and she gripped the edge of the dresser. "Get out," she rasped.

He cursed with more imagination than she'd ever heard in her life, and ran agitated fingers through his hair. "I'm sorry I said that, Megan. You made me so angry—"

"Get out," she repeated firmly.

He took several steps toward her, but she gave him a venomous look that stopped him stock still in his tracks. "You know I didn't mean it."

She snorted a laugh. "Yes, you did."

"I was angry, Megan!"

"So am I, angrier than I've ever been in my life. Not at you, but at myself. Why I didn't keep my mouth shut about Clancey and let you get your just desserts I'll never know. Now, get out!"

In one sweeping motion he picked up the rest of his clothes. "I'll leave you alone for a while to cool off. I'm going to call Atlanta, but I'll be back, and then we'll sit down and finish this discussion calmly."

He went through the sliding glass doors, wearing only underwear and carrying his pants and shirt. The vague thought crossed her mind that neither could appreciate the humor of the situation now. When he returned to her room, she intended to be far away. Indeed, she felt deadly serious.

The story made the newspapers the next morning. Megan couldn't avoid learning about it when Arlene rushed in waving a copy of the *Atlanta Constitution.* "Have you read this?"

Megan didn't think she could stand any more emotional blows, but her heart twisted with pain for the man she once again told herself she despised. It was all there—how his disenchanted employee had taken all the work already done on the heretofore secret ad campaign for the burgeoning airline and handed it over to the executives of Powell Associates with their promise of an outlandishly high increase over what Josh was paying him.

The reporter, as Megan thought reporters were inclined to do, painted Josh's future as blacker even than it would probably be and hinted at overindulgences such as women and booze as the causes of his lack of astuteness.

Josh's only quoted remark—and Megan suspected it was his only quotable comment—was, "I'll have something to say when the deal is complete."

She looked at the picture of the man who scowled up at her from the newspaper and smoothed her finger over it as though to erase the lines of worry from his face. There was no sense in wishing away the emptiness she felt inside. It only yawned wider.

She had packed her bags the moment Josh had retreated to his room. She had stuffed all the clothes she'd so carefully folded into the bags, dressed hurriedly, and, looking to see that she'd left nothing behind, gone to the check-in desk at Seascape.

Getting someone to drive her to the airport had been no problem. Even the paper work involved in renting a car for the rest of the trip home was handled smoothly. Or was it that she was so immersed in her heartache that she didn't notice the hassles?

With every mile that had clicked off between Hilton Head and Atlanta, she'd sworn that she hated Josh. He had mocked her, insulted her, made something sordid out of the splendor they'd shared, cheapened her unrestrained, loving responses to him.

But by the time she reached her dark, lonely house, she admitted that she'd provoked him to say what he had. It would have been so easy to reasonably suggest that he call Barnes himself and have him repeat verbatim what Clancey had said. Josh could have evaluated it himself. Maybe Barnes *had* been overreacting.

But she hadn't made such a suggestion. She had let pride and stubbornness blind her once again. At his first sign of indifference to her news, she'd gotten her back up. Once that happened, Lord help anyone who tried to dissuade her from the position she'd taken.

God help Josh, was her prayer all week. The newspaper accounts grew less informative, and by Wednesday they disappeared altogether. Then she had to rely on the grapevine for information. Filtering rumor from truth became a time- and energy-consuming enterprise, but she was eager to hear the latest developments.

"I think Clancey is seeing the error of his ways," Barnes told Megan and Jo Hampson at the coffee machine. "Seems the folks at Air South aren't convinced that Powell can carry off the campaign with the panache that Bennett can. Clancey's hearing his own death knell."

As Megan left them to return to her office, she heard Barnes say, "Hey, Jo, how about dinner some night?"

Megan's lips lifted into a smile, which seemed to be rare these days.

Time dragged by as she waded through the paper work that had collected during her brief absence. At night, exhausted but unable to sleep, she longed for Josh. She cursed her body's aching need for him. He flitted in and out of her mind in glorious memories of their days together at Hilton Head. She saw him in every attitude—teasing her as he dragged her into the ocean, his eyes alight with mischief; laughing, his head thrown back, his eyes shining with delight as they sailed over the ground in the swing; languorous, as they lay enmeshed on her bed, his eyes glassy with the aftermath of loving her.

Somehow she made it through the week.

She arrived home late Friday evening after battling traffic that, had it been choreographed, couldn't have become more entangled. Shrugging gratefully out of her clothes and pulling on a thin cotton robe that zipped up the front, she padded barefoot into the kitchen to eat the pizza she'd ill-advisedly crossed six lanes of traffic to pick up.

"Damn." As she pulled the top of the cardboard box away, the mozzarella she'd paid an extra dollar for stuck to it. It was the proverbial last straw. Dropping dejectedly into a chair, she laid her head on the butcher-block table and wept.

Her thin shoulders shook convulsively; tears coursed down her cheeks. She wept for the husband she hadn't loved enough, for the man she loved now. She cried for their lost love. She wept because she couldn't go to him now, when he needed her most.

Mascara dripped onto the surface of the table, and she smeared it even more when she tried to wipe it up with her hand. "What the hell difference does it make?" she sobbed. "Who ever sees it?"

"Did you say something?"

She spun around on the chair seat, fear clutching in her throat at the low, masculine voice. Josh was leaning against the doorjamb. His face looked almost as ravaged as hers must. There were dark circles under his eyes, his cheeks seemed sunken, and his rakish brow had lost some of it's cockiness. His suit coat was slung over one shoulder and held there by a crooked index finger. His vest hung open. White shirt sleeves were rolled to his elbows and his tie was loosened. It gave her a vague sense of comfort to know that Joshua Bennett's clothes could wrinkle just like anyone else's.

She swiped at the tears on her face and stood up slowly. For once she didn't bristle, didn't squawk. She didn't demand to know what he was doing there. She did exactly what she wanted to do.

She walked into his arms.

They came around her like a protective cloak and hugged her tight. For long moments they clung to each other, not speaking, not kissing, not caressing, only rocking together. She imbibed his strength. He was what she wanted.

"Why were you crying?" he asked at long last, taking her face between his palms.

"My pizza," she said, gesturing offhandedly.

A corner of his mouth twitched. As she had been all week, he seemed unable to smile. After a moment he tried it again, and grinned narrowly. "What's wrong with it?"

He maneuvered them backward toward the table, sliding his feet, careful not to step on her bare toe. He lifted the box top and saw the damage. He made a regretful sound, then pinched off a string of the cheese and popped it into his mouth. "Salvageable. Maybe." He swallowed noisily and coaxed a smile from her trembling lips. "Why were you crying?" he asked again. His eyes probed hers, searching for answers.

"For me."

"Why?"

"I'm abysmally unhappy."

"Why?"

"The man I love is going through a very difficult time and I'm afraid he wouldn't want my offer to help him in any way I can."

"What an arrogant ass he is. As a matter of fact I think someone once called him that. Why wouldn't he want your help?"

"Because the last time I saw him I said things to him that shouldn't have been said."

"He said something too. Something ugly. No one would blame you for despising the jerk."

"He didn't mean it. I know he didn't." She drew in a breath that rippled like a sob. "I should have been standing by him this week, supporting him, helping him."

Josh crushed her against him and, bending from his great height, laid his head on her shoulder. His nose burrowed in the silky hollow of her throat. "You tried, my love, you tried. I wouldn't listen and you were right. I was so damned sure of my own power." His arms squeezed as though to impress her into his body. "I need you, Megan."

His head came up, and his amber eyes studied each feature of her face intently. "I've never said that to another human being in my life," he admitted. "I've never confessed to needing anyone or anything, but I need you."

Her hands clasped the sides of his head, and she

threaded her fingers through his dark hair. "I need you too. I need you to cure me of stubbornness and pride."

"Pride." He shook his head in self-deprecation. "I could give you lessons in having too much pride. I've had a chip on my shoulder since I was about ten years old, and the harder someone tried to knock it off, the larger it grew. What I wanted I went after. Come hell or high water, I got it. I just couldn't give you up. I had to have you."

He took one of her hands from his hair and kissed the palm. "But winning you isn't worth your despising me in the process. You won't have to give up one thing in your life for me. I swear it. Not your career, not your ambition, nothing. Just be a part of my life. Please."

"I wanted to despise you from the first moment I met you, because you saw right through me. More than that, you were always ready to point out my shortcomings."

"For pure meanness, just to get a reaction out of you. Anger was better than nothing."

"It was always a sweet anger."

His eyebrow had regained some of its confidence and curved upward. "Sounds a lot like love to me."

She leaned toward him provocatively. "Why don't you kiss me and find out?"

He needed no second invitation. His mouth opened over hers, and his tongue delved inside with rapacious need. It scoured her mouth, taking away all the bitterness that had risen between them, and leaving behind only the sweet taste of their love.

"Where's the bedroom?" he asked out of the corner of his mouth.

She pointed in the general direction, and he urged her to lead him. "How did you get in?" she asked, unfastening the buttons of his shirt as she walked backward in front of him.

"Through the door. Later I'm going to give you a lecture on leaving it unlocked." He raked her with a lewd look. "Any sex fiend could come walking in here."

On the brink of a laugh, she stopped abruptly. "Josh, what about Air South and Powell?"

"I'm mad as hell at the whole bunch. If it weren't for them, I'd have been here Sunday night. By the way, remind me to give you another lecture about sneaking out of resorts, renting a car, and driving alone across the whole state of Georgia."

He was pushing her inexorably toward the bedroom. "But what about Air South?" she asked.

His sigh was one of weary surrender when her heels dug into the deep carpet. "I've been in boardrooms all—"

"Bedrooms?"

"*Board*rooms."

"Just checking. Proceed."

He gave her a withering look. "Just for that crack, I'm not going to tell you anything else now except to say that, by Monday or Tuesday at the latest, the newspaper reporters who had me dead and buried will be forced to write retractions."

"I have every confidence in you," Megan said, coming up on her tiptoes and looping her arms around his neck.

With their mouths fused and their bodies melded together, his hands curved under her bottom and lifted her off the floor as he carried her the rest of the way into the guest bedroom. He knew she would have felt uncomfortable with him in the room she had shared with James, and her heart overflowed with love. How could she have ever thought him insensitive?

He set her down slowly, and she slid against him, meeting the hard urgency of his desire on her descent. Lifting heavy eyelids, she looked up at him bewitchingly. She peeled the vest off his shoulders and dropped it to the floor. She slipped the tie over his head and began taking off his shirt. He eased off his shoes with the toe of one foot on the heel of the other and kicked them aside.

When his shirt had joined the heap of clothes on the floor, she ran her fingers through the mat of hair on his chest. Her sensitive fingertips fluttered over his nipples, which sprang to life, growing erect beneath her touch. With deliberate leisure, she leaned forward to kiss him. Her tongue batted against him lightly. "Do you like that?" she whispered.

"Find out," he challenged.

She laid the back of her hand on his chest and slid it down slowly until her fingers went past his belt and into his trousers. He smiled smugly when she raised naughty eyes to his. Closing a fist around his buckle, she began backing toward the double bed, dragging him with her.

"You're going to marry me, aren't you?" she asked.

"Will you greet me at the door every night in a sheer robe with nothing on underneath?"

"How did you know?"

"I could see your nipples," he said softly. "And a shadowy hint of this." His hand touched the top of her thighs with the overabundance of arrogance she'd always accused him of having.

She could only sigh his name as a familiar liquid fire began to seep through her body at his touch. She sat down on the side of the bed while he rid himself of pants and underwear.

When he was standing before her with the magnificence of his form revealed, she rested her hands on the slight curve of his waist and leaned forward to press her lips against the silky shaft of hair that pointed down his abdomen. Her head moved, nose nuzzling, lips nibbling. Her tongue danced over his navel and beyond . . .

Her name came out of his throat like a prayer, and he dropped to his knees beside the bed. "I've got to love you. For the rest of my life, I'll love you. This is the way it should have been years ago."

"It couldn't be then."

"But it will be more precious to us now."

He began by taking her hand and kissing the palm as he would her mouth. His lips opened over the soft flesh and deflowered it with his thrusting tongue. He slid it along each finger with agonizing slowness, then caught the fingertip in his mouth and sucked it like a candy stick.

"Please, Josh," she cried, reaching for his shoulder with her free hand.

He eluded her grasp. "Let me love you like I wanted to the first time. Slowly. Fully." He used both hands to pull down the zipper of her robe. With reverence, he lowered it from her shoulders as though uncovering a sacred treasure.

His eyes worshiped her first, surveying her like a rare piece of sculpture created for him alone. Lifting up first one arm, then the other, he kissed the insides of her elbows, finding erogenous places she didn't know she possessed.

He tugged on the nipples of her breasts while his hands coasted down her ribs. With his thumbs, he massaged the downy mound between her legs with the same erotic rhythm as his tongue circling her nipples.

She grabbed handfuls of his dark hair and imprisoned his head against her breasts. He wrested himself free. "Shhh, not yet. Lie down."

She had no energy to argue as he gently set her down. Her head tossed frantically on the pillow as his mouth continued its ritual on her stomach, working ever downward.

Long moments passed while she swirled through a galaxy of uncharted bliss. It was all the better when he covered her body with his and tightly sheathed himself in the depths of her love. They soared above one universe and went on to the next, each one higher and brighter, until they reached that plane where spirits are united in an everlasting fire of love.

Replete, they clung together, marveling over the magnitude of the love they shared.

"I've been selfish again. Forgive me for taking my time," he said quietly.

"There's one thing I hope you'll always be fiercely selfish about—your love for me," she whispered.

He smiled and cuddled her close against him. "Of that you may be sure, my love. Of that you may be sure."

More
Sandra Brown!

Please turn this page
for a
bonus excerpt
from

SWEET ANGER

available
wherever books are sold.

W e've got a two-alarm fire working on Clermont just south of Sixth Avenue. It should be at about 42H on your Mapsco. And get there pronto. I want some good video."

The inch-long ash on the end of Pinkie Lewis's cigarette fell unnoticed on his battered, cluttered, littered desk. The harried news director paused long enough to say "Hiya, sweetheart" to the young woman who had just moved aside a day-old Moon Pie, a roll of masking tape, and two cups of cold gray coffee in order to perch on the corner of the desk.

"When you're done with the fire," Pinkie went on, returning his attention to the two men lounging by his desk, "swing by that elementary school where the third-graders are writing letters to the Russians. If we have any time left on the six o'clock, it'll make good human interest. Anybody hear from Jack lately? It's taken him four hours to shoot that bit on the drug bust."

"Maybe he's hanging around, hoping they'll let him sample the goods." The videotape photographer grinned as he heaved the camera to his shoulder. The reporter, who was pulling on his sport coat, thought his cohort's suggestion was funny and laughed.

"I'll have his ass," Pinkie growled. "So what are you two bozos waiting for?" The grins collapsed. That particular tone in Pinkie's voice could bring about miraculous changes in a man. "The damn fire will be out before you get there. I want to see flames, smoke, tragedy in the making," he yelled, waving his arms descriptively. "Now get out of here!"

The reporter and cameraman left, stumbling in their haste. Pinkie glowered after them and ran a hand through his hair. Or he would have if he'd had any hair. Actually, he ran his hand over a rapidly growing bald spot that blended into his beefy forehead. It was his florid complexion and fair hair that had given him his nickname.

"One of these days you're going to have a heart attack," the young woman commented. Disgustedly she stubbed out three cigarette butts left in the ashtray. They hadn't been properly ground out and were curling acrid smoke into the already polluted atmosphere of the television newsroom.

"Naw. I drink too much whiskey. It scares sickness off." Pinkie picked up a Styrofoam cup and took a swig. He made a face at the stale coffee. "Buy you a cup," he said, taking the woman's arm and guiding her into the hall and toward an alcove where numerous vending machines were tucked outside of the flow of continuous foot traffic.

As usual, Pinkie's pockets produced no change when he began slapping them in search. "Let me buy this time," Kari Stewart said, smiling. The coffee was too black and bitter, but it was hot. Crossing her ankles, she leaned against the wall and sipped cautiously.

Pinkie smiled at her with paternal affection. "Godamighty, you're a sight for sore eyes. Helluva day. One of the video cameras is on the blink. It'll cost a fortune to repair and then I'll catch hell for going over budget. I've got two unexciting but dependable reporters out with flu." He belched. "I need a drink."

"You need a hot, balanced meal, far fewer cigarettes, far less whiskey—"

"Yes, Mother—"

"—and a good woman to take care of you."

"Oh, yeah?" Pinkie asked belligerently. This was a familiar topic of conversation. "You got someone in mind?"

"Bonnie."

"That dried-up old prune! She's too old for me."

Kari laughed. The switchboard operator who handled all the calls coming into the television station with amazing alacrity and patience had carried a torch for the crusty news director for years. "You'll never change, Pinkie. You're biased, stubborn, grouchy, and predictable. That's why I love you." She poked him in the spare tire that sagged over his belt.

"How'd the interview go?"

"He was as wretched as he's reputed to be." That morning Kari had interviewed an aging television sit-com actor who was now doing "legitimate theater" on the dinner theater circuit. "I can see why his varied series went down the tubes. He was rude, obnoxious, and condescending. But I'll have the last laugh. I went to last night's rehearsal. The production is a turkey. And I didn't think anyone could ruin a perfectly wonderful Neil Simon."

Pinkie crumpled his empty cup and tossed it in the general direction of the trash can. It didn't make it, but he didn't notice. "Goose the old geezer right in the pride. Don't soft-soap it. I want gutsy stuff on the newscast, even during your entertainment segment."

Kari saluted. "Right, Chief."

Pinkie's beet-red face split into a grin as he lit one of his unfiltered cigarettes. "And *that's* what I love about you. You don't give me any guff." He sauntered away in the direction of the newsroom. "And you've got great legs," he called over his shoulder.

Kari took the compliment for what it was, a teasing gesture between friends. Pinkie had been her friend and ally ever since she'd signed on with WBTV five years ago. Where others were cowed by the querulous news director, Kari, as a green intern with no more television journalism experience than her college diploma afforded her, had called his bluff one day and forever won his respect. She talked to him as no one else would dare and got away with it because of their mutual affection. She knew he wasn't nearly as fierce as he pretended.

Pinkie saw in her a dedicated, thorough reporter with initiative. He could count on her not to "screw up," as he put it. At the same time, he liked her warm personality, her femininity. He had had a hunch that the viewers would be as charmed as he, and he had been proven right.

When Kari had married Thomas Wynne two years earlier, Pinkie had feared he would lose her. But she had assured him that she wanted to continue working. "Thomas agrees. Until we decide to start a family, he wants me to do anything I want. And I want to keep working for you."

"There might be a conflict of interests here, Kari," Pinkie had said. "How can you impartially cover the city hall beat when your husband is one of the city councilmen?"

"I've already thought of that. Much as I hate giving up that beat, I think it's the proper thing to do."

"So where does that leave us?"

"I've got an idea for an entertainment segment on the news programs."

His white eyebrows had jumped up then lowered into a thoughtful frown. "Let's hash it over."

Pinkie had trusted her judgment and her ability to implement her idea successfully. Kari Stewart's critiques were a highlight of every newscast. She was witty and incisive without being scathing or vicious. The viewers adored her.

Now Kari went into the editing room and closed

the door behind her. She dropped into the chair and fished a cartridge of videotape from her oversized bag, which served as both purse and carryall. Pushing back a mass of untamed blond hair from her cheek, she inserted the cartridge into the computerized editing console and began watching the interview she had conducted barely an hour before.

She picked up the telephone and dialed an extension. "Sam, hi, Kari. Can you bring that tape you shot last night of the rehearsal to editing room three, please? Thanks."

A few moments later the door opened behind her and she said, "Just set it down, Sam. Thanks. I'm using that for B-roll. I'll be ready for it in a minute."

She was capably punching buttons while scanning the two monitors, one with the unedited tape playing, the other with the edited version she was electronically compiling. She was so engrossed that she didn't notice that the door didn't close.

"Kari."

Pinkie's voice and the unfamiliar tone of it brought her head around. She had seen him in moods ranging from elation when they had scooped all their competitors on a story, to drunken melancholia over a bad ratings report. She had never seen him as he was now: deflated, sagging, abject, and most uncharacteristic of all, pale.

She half rose out of her chair. "Pinkie? What is it?" He laid a hand on her shoulder and eased her gently back into the chair.

"An accident report came in over the police radio a few minutes ago."

"And?" A cold fist of dread began squeezing her heart. "What kind of accident?"

He ran his hand over his head, then dragged it down his face, distorting the features. "Auto/pedestrian. Just a few blocks from here, right downtown. I sent a cameraman over there. He just called in."

She did stand now, fighting off his hands as he tried to restrain her. "Thomas? Something's happened to Thomas?" There was no one else in her life. Pinkie wouldn't be acting like this if it weren't Thomas.

She made a mad dash for the door, but Pinkie caught her. "It is Thomas, Kari."

"He's hurt? What happened? What?"

"A truck hit him."

"Oh, my God."

Pinkie dropped his eyes to the middle of her chest, which was just about eye level for him. "It was . . . fatal. He died at the scene. I'm sorry, sweetheart."

Several ponderous seconds ticked by. She remained motionless, speechless. Disbelief paralyzed her. Then quietly she said, "You're telling me Thomas is dead?" Her hands gripped Pinkie's shirtfront like claws and she shook him. "A truck hit him?! Killed him?!" she screamed. Several of the station's employees were now crowded into the doorway of the editing room. The women were weeping. The men looked distinctly uncomfortable.

"Kari, Kari," Pinkie crooned. He patted her back.

"There's a mistake. It couldn't be—"

"I made the reporter confirm it a dozen times before I came to tell you." Her eyes were wild in her pallid face. Her lips worked, but no sound came out. "Come on," Pinkie said gently. "They've taken him to Denver General. I'll drive you."

It was the cold that struck her first. She had never been in a room this cold. The dual swinging doors closed silently behind her and Pinkie as they entered. She shrank against him, hating this stark, clinical place instantly.

The fluorescent lights hurt her eyes. The brightness offended her. Shouldn't this room be dark and serene, lending death some dignity and reverence? But here death was considered only a physical phenomenon. This place was so very sterile. And so very cold.

She felt like turning to run, but Pinkie urged her forward. A man in a white lab coat looked up from his desk. He stood up immediately "Mrs. Wynne?"

"Yes."

He led them to a large table draped with a white sheet. Beneath the sheet lay the still form of a man. Kari began to whimper involuntarily and mashed her lips flat with her fingers.

How could she bear to see Thomas's body mangled and bloodied? Would she disgrace him and herself by her actions? Would she scream? Faint? Dissolve into hysterics?

The pathologist pulled back the sheet.

At first she thought it must all be a tasteless joke someone was playing on her. Or some outlandish mistake. Her eyes flew up to the man holding the sheet. He read the unspoken question in them; saw her incredulity.

"He was killed by the impact," he said softly. "The truck struck him from behind. The trauma traveled up his spine into his brain. There is a bruise on his back. Otherwise . . ."

He left the rest unfinished.

Kari stared down at Thomas's body. He looked as though he were asleep. Nothing more. His face was relaxed. The silver hair that she had found so attractive the first time she met him was neatly combed. The hand lying by his side looked merely at rest, ready to lift up a tennis racquet or caress her hair.

His tall body seemed as strong as it had that morning when she had kissed him good-bye. He exercised religiously at a gymnasium to maintain that hard muscle tone and to avoid middle-age spread.

"Thomas, Thomas, darling." Her whisper sounded loud in the silent room. She almost expected him to open his eyes and look up at her, to say her name, to smile. She would see again the sparkle in his blue eyes and hear the rich sound of his laugh.

She had thought it would be unbearable to see his body broken. It was almost worse to see it looking so normal. His untouched state made the whole thing seem that much more absurd and unreal. It simply hadn't happened!

But it had. He was horrifyingly still.

"Where would you like us to send him?"

"Send him?" she repeated vacantly.

"I'll telephone you later," Pinkie said to the man. "Mrs. Wynne hasn't had time to make her arrangements."

"I understand." The pathologist began to lower the sheet.

"Wait!" she cried. The word echoed eerily off the tile walls. She couldn't leave him. Not in this terrible place. Not in this cold, cold room. If she left him lying here, his face covered by the sheet, it would be official. She couldn't cope with that yet. She couldn't admit that Thomas, her husband, was dead.

"Kari, you have to go." Pinkie laid gentle hands on her shoulders.

"Thomas." Her eyes filled with tears that rolled heavily down her cheeks. Tentatively she stretched her fingers toward him. She touched his hair, his forehead.

Then, sobbing uncontrollably, she collapsed into Pinkie's arms. He led her out.

It was unexpected, unheard of, bizarre. The day of the accident had been clear. For some undetermined reason, the driver of the delivery truck had lost control as he turned the corner. The truck had swerved, jumped the curb, and robbed Denver of one of its leading citizens and Kari Stewart Wynne of her husband. He had been walking back to the courthouse after a luncheon appointment. Innocently. Feeling the false sense of security human beings are wont to feel about their mortality. He had died instantly of the impact.

Kari stared at the flower-blanketed casket and wondered how it was possible that Thomas, her vibrant, dynamic husband, was sealed lifelessly inside.

She gripped Pinkie's hand. He had been a bulwark for the last two days, seeing to the myriad details while she moved in a daze. She was grateful for this mental netherland she moved in. It protected her from reality. Without it, she wouldn't have been able to cope.

She had no parents to lean on for support. Her mother had died when Kari was a child. Her father, whom she had adored and admired, had died just before she graduated from college with her degree in communications.

And now Thomas had been taken from her, too.

She went through the rites of burial feeling nothing but a deep hollowness inside her. It was only when she was returning home, riding in Pinkie's car with him and Bonnie, that she began to weep. Bonnie silently passed her a box of tissues.

"Do you remember when we got married?" Kari asked them rhetorically. "People were shocked." Her voice, she noted, was husky. Maybe she had cried more than she remembered.

"People are always shocked when a couple doesn't fit the norm. There was over thirty years difference in your ages," Pinkie said.

"Thirty-two years to be exact. But I never felt there was any difference."

"Thomas didn't look as old as he was. He certainly didn't live like most men in their sixties."

Kari smiled at Bonnie. "No, he didn't." She turned her gaze out the window. It surprised her to see so much activity. To most people this was an ordinary workday. Life was going on.

"I was distraught over my father's death," she said reflectively. "I remember coming to work at WBTV with the sole intention of making that my life's focus. My work was going to be all I lived for. Then I met Thomas. He gave purpose to my life again. I don't know what I would have done without him. We were so happy." She sighed. "Is fate jealous of one's happiness?"

"Sometimes I think it is," Bonnie said kindly. "You're beautiful and talented. Thomas Wynne was rich and successful. The two of you seemed to have it all."

"We did," Kari confirmed as Pinkie turned his car into the lane that led up to the house she had shared with Thomas. "Please come in."

To read more, look for *Sweet Anger*
by Sandra Brown.

SANDRA BROWN is the author of over sixty books, of which over fifty were *New York Times* bestsellers, including the #1 *New York Times* bestseller *The Alibi, The Crush, Envy, The Switch, Standoff, Unspeakable, Fat Tuesday, Exclusive, The Witness, Charade, Where There's Smoke,* and *French Silk.* Her novels have been published in more than thirty languages. She and her husband live in Texas.